FORBIDDEN KISS
(Julian's Mate)

By: A. R. Flowers

Copyright © 2014 A. R. Flowers
All Rights Reserved.
ISBN #13:978-0989976510
ISBN #10:0989976513
Editor: J. Nanton

COVER BY: SelfPubBookCovers.com/Roman

Dedication

To my beloved son, Quentin, who will always be missed, but never forgotten. You are forever in my heart.

Acknowledgements

A very special thank you to my editor, J. Nanton, who works hard to see that all of this is put together with precision.

Thank you to all of my co-workers who continue to support me in this endeavor. You know who you are.

To my sisters and my brother and other family members, thanks for your support.

Mom, thank you for your continued support!!

A special thanks to my bestie Annie McNeill. Thank you for always being there.

Contents

Chapter 1

Trinity was startled awake from the same bad dream she had been having for the last three months, looked at the clock on her night table. The red numbers blinked 2:30am. Her dream was so vivid; someone was chasing her, she was running and looking back over her shoulder. She was also calling out the name of her boyfriend, Colin. She kept calling his name but he didn't hear her, wouldn't hear her. He was running too, but away from her. Someone, no, something was after her and she had to get away. She was surrounded by dark, then seeing the faces of her parents and brothers. Suddenly, out of nowhere, he appeared. Whoever he was, he was tall and broad with a deep voice. With his outstretched arms, he pointed toward her direction telling her to come to him. I will protect you, come to me Trinity; come to me and you will be safe. I won't let anyone hurt you. I won't let anyone touch you. You are mine.

As Trinity looked around again, she wondered where Colin had gone and more importantly, who was this man, and how did he know her name. What did he want to protect her from? Why was the family in this particular dream? They hadn't been in any of the others. What's happening? The dreams wouldn't be so bad if they were dreams about having sex, but this. This is too much.

"If this doesn't stop, I may need to visit my doctor, she thought."

"Maybe, Dr. Marshall can give me something to help me sleep through the night, or at least help me make some sense of my dreams." "I'll call Dr. Jane and make an appointment for later in the week," Trinity said to herself.

The day had been tranquil and clear, but now the sun was setting to a beautiful hue. Trinity Parker had just left home for work. Little did she know she would never see her parents again.

Since their spirited days of adolescence, James and Eden Parker were inseparable. So, it was no surprise to their families when they announced their engagement and finally wed. They had three wonderful children—Simon, Trinity, and Scott—who loved them dearly. James and Eden Parker did everything together. They took flying lessons together, became pilots together; they were experienced pilots. The Parkers were a happy and affectionate family and remained so until the day of the plane crash, which took their lives, and turned the Parker siblings' world up-side-down.

James had a lucrative textile business in Rhode Island. The day of the crash, he had been in negotiations with his partners to sell off the business. James and Eden Parker were supposed to spend half the day dealing with company business and the rest of the evening was to be a romantic one just for the two of them.

The sky was very crisp and clear that morning. It was a great day for flying. James had filed a flight plan and was cleared for takeoff. Not long after James circled and left the airport, signals started going off in the plane.

James signaled a mayday, but it was too late. The plane fell off the radar. Smoke could be seen as far as ten miles away. James and Eden Parker were gone.

The Parker children and other family and friends were devastated. Trinity more so. She looked t her mother for guidance and advice. She was close to both of her parents but she felt closer to her mother.

The day of the funeral, many of the Parker's friends and relatives were in attendance, as well as those Mr. Parker was in commerce with. The service was short but beautiful.

Two days later, the will was read by the family lawyer. In accordance with the will of Mr. and Mrs. Parker, all of the cash and stock was to be divided between the three children. Trinity would be the sole owner of the textile company to do with it as she wished. The shares held by James Parker's business partners would remain theirs, along with a bonus to be released to them.

Scott's money was to be put into a Trust Fund until he reached the age of twenty-one. Simon had plans to expand his furniture business and Trinity decided to seek the advice of an attorney to help her in dealing with the sale of the textile company. She did not want to leave everything in the hands of the lawyer that her parents had, she just didn't trust Giles Butler. She couldn't say why; maybe, it was the shady way he always gawked at her.

As a teenager, Trin--the nickname her mother gave her --had lived in a modest home with her brothers in the suburb of New York. Her family had moved there from Rhode Island, where James Parker owned a textile company and the business was a profitable one. She moved back home to take care of her younger brother Scott, who was just beginning high school when their parents died. Her older brother Simon, who also lived in the city with his girlfriend Alex, decided to come back and stay on weekends to help out as well.

Simon was a playboy while in high school and throughout college. He worked for his father in a small office in the city while in college and decided he wanted to open up his own high end furniture shop to those who could afford the sticker price. Simon relocated to the city, where he met Alex. Not long afterward, they started dating and within a couple of months, she moved in.

Trin was now a beautiful woman of twenty-four with a curvy body, long silky sexy legs, sensuous pouty downturned lips, shoulder length raven hair and the most stunning steel blue eyes. However, growing up was hard for her. She had always kept to herself in school. Introversion, being her primary problem, was one of the reasons the popular girls, Courtney and Vicki, would pick on her, make fun of her clothes, and how she wore her hair. She had the biggest crush on Jason Foster since high school. Jason was the quarterback of their football team and was dating Courtney— one of the popular girls—along with Vicki, from time to time. The one bright spot in her social life was that she became friends with Sara Arnold, the new girl in the neighborhood. Sara moved in next door about a month after school started. Sara was not the shy type. She could easily have become one of the established girls in school. She had an outgoing personality and dressed the part. Her parents were moderately wealthy social butterflies. They entertained every weekend. When the girls first met, they knew they would be best friends.

High school graduation came and went. Afterwards, Jason's family moved to California where he attended college. Kellan spent his time between Vicki and some of the other girls from school, until one day Vicki saw Kellan with Sara Arnold; that was the end of their relationship.

They all went to the local university. Trin's reputation, as an unattractive shy girl, followed her throughout college. She was shunned by some of her classmates. Sara tried dressing her in fashionable clothes and fixing her hair only to have her go back to her own style.

"You're hopeless, Trinity," Sara said."

"No, I'm not."

"I'm just being me." Trinity said. "I just want to get my degree and learn the business world," she stated as she ran her fingers through her hair."

"Well, in order to do that, you need to dress like you're in this century," Sara said.

The girls stared at each other, and then burst into a fit of laughter.

Trin and Sara met Lisa while in management class. They became fast friends and were almost inseparable. Lisa was the mother hen of their cliché. She was always quiet though, unless someone ruffled her feathers. The class watched her shut this guy down one day. He was talking to his classroom chums and making fun of the way Trinity was dressed, and how she wanted him (which was a lie); nevertheless, that was the last time he said anything disdainful to the three of them, especially in front of Lisa.

Trinity finally changed the way she dressed, fixed her hair and even wore makeup. While in college, they landed jobs at the Palace, an upscale restaurant in the city. They started out as waitresses working weekends and some evenings.

After graduation, Vicki went to California to become a model. Kellan landed a job in his father's firm as an editor. Trinity put her business management degree and skills to good use. She worked her way up the ladder to the position of assistant manager and was running the Palace as her own business. She aspires that someday it will be. Sara was promoted to cocktail waitress and Lisa now works as the hostess.

Trinity, Sara and Lisa saved their money and moved into the city. They each lived in their own apartment, within the same building. Each apartment had two huge bedrooms, a bathroom large enough to put a bed in, a moderate sized walk-in closet, a cozy living room with fire place, and a kitchen with all modern appliances. Trinity fell in love with her new place. Her next purchase was her first car with her well earned money. She was now on her way.

Having to move back to the suburbs made Trinity feel out of place. She didn't want to lose the independence she had gained with living on her own. She couldn't have a personal life living here with her brother. After all, she was seeing someone special, Colin, the family lawyer's son. Giles rarely talked about family, as far as anyone knew, Giles Butler had a wife and two dogs, they took long vacations out of the country twice a year and it had been that way for what seemed like forever.

Trin jumped when the phone rang, although she was expecting a call from her employer, Marcellus about the manager's position she interviewed for just two days prior. She was confident that she would be chosen. She wanted the position badly. After all, that's what she studied in college and worked her way towards. The phone conversation lasted all of five minutes and when she hung up; the house came alive with a loud squeal.

Colin came into the restaurant nightly to see the woman he was dating. He was a fairly handsome man of twenty-five, at least six and a half feet tall, broad shoulders, sharp features, pale blue eyes and a head full of wavy blond hair. Their relationship was good, they had sex regularly. Colin, a hi-tech whiz kid, was owner of a Fortune 500 computer chip company with a branch office in Denver.

He stayed through Trin's shift and drove her home, with every intention of getting laid. Trinity gave her car keys to Lisa so that she and Sara could get home. They closed up and walked out of the restaurant together with Colin waiting to see that they were in the car and had pulled off, and then he and Trinity walked to his car. He opened the door and waited until she was seated, then closed it, walked around to the driver's side, hopped in, pulled Trinity into his arms and kissed her passionately.

"I want you so bad I could take you here in this car," he said."

"Climb in the back seat and let me have a little taste of your honey."

"Whoa! Colin, not here. Keep your tongue in your mouth and your cock in your pants until you get me home," she replied.

Colin scratched his ear and said, "I've missed you these last few days. I was hoping to have wrapped up my business meetings more swiftly. Everybody had problems, which is why it took me so long to get back."

"I know, Colin, I missed you too," Trinity said.
"Your calls were so short, but I understand. Did you get to see any interesting parts of Denver?" Trin asked.

"No, that's not why I went there," Colin said bluntly, his voice full of bitterness.

"I don't do sightseeing, you know that."

"Well, did you find out who was hacking into your computers out there?" she asked.

"No, but we have some leads. I've hired a private firm to look into it. So, I can spend more time with you," he said.

The minute the car was parked, Colin rushed them into the apartment building, almost knocking down two people on the elevator. As soon as they exited the elevator, he all but pushed Trinity through the front door to the apartment. Without saying one word, he dragged her to the bedroom and planted his lips on her mouth. It took him all of ten seconds to get undressed, ripping off his shirt then stepping out of his shoes and pulling down his pants. The only thing she could do was sit and stare at him.

Colin was definitely in a hurry, he said nothing as he grabbed her feet and pulled her down the bed. With one hand, he began to fondle himself until he was hard and made sure she was wet enough with the other. Colin climbed on top of her fully clothed body, positioned himself between her legs then slammed into her. His grinding started to irritate her. He picked up the pace for about two more thrusts; then went still. With a grunt, he came. It was obvious to him that she had not gotten there yet. He played with her clit—circling with his finger and licking— until she came, leaving her breathless and slightly ruddy-faced. It was the first time she had experienced anything like this with Colin. It was as though he had become a different person, he was a hunter and she his prey. After they unwound, Trinity undressed and he gently caressed her body, sucking on her breasts and licking around her ear. They had sex again, the way they normally did, quiet and reserved.

Colin didn't spend the night, he left around four in the morning, stressing about having to get up early and go into the office for a conference call.

Later that morning, the girls got together in Trin's apartment for breakfast; since, she was the better cook. Sitting at the kitchen table, Lisa looked over at her friends then addressed Trinity,

"How did it go last night?"

"Since we discuss everything, I'll tell you."

"At first he was really aggressive, but that changed on the second round and he was as gentle as a lamb in bed. We don't have the earth shattering sex I have been hoping for. He grunts, I grunt, we orgasm, that's it," Trinity said,

Feeling uncomfortable discussing her intimacy.

"Girl, you need a man who's going to make you see stars, feel your toes curl and your eyes cross and much more," Lisa said.

"Well, when you find one, let me know," Trin answered.

They all laughed behind Lisa's comment. They ate then Lisa and Sara went back to their own apartments promising to meet again later for dinner.

She thought back to the last few times Colin and her had sex, because it definitely wasn't making love. She felt as though something was lacking and that there should be more to what she was getting. She thought she was giving her all, but apparently somebody in this relationship wasn't. In short, she wanted more and desired more, but how to get it was the big question.

Chapter 2

There was no place in the city like the Palace. It was a remarkably upscale restaurant, beautifully refurbished to resemble a Victorian house. To be short, nothing compared to it. The atmosphere inside was warm and inviting; furthermore, it boasted countless types of cuisine, floor to ceiling windows, a panoramic view from the inside, outdoor seating, privacy booths on the second level for those who wished to be unobserved, exceptional serving areas, a wet bar that encompasses half the room, and a spectacular open floor for dancing. The Palace was the venue to be seen on a Saturday night by film and stage stars, some producers, musicians, and other celebrities or the occasional wannabe hoping to catch the eye of someone in the business.

Trin picked up the phone on the third ring.

"Hello."

"Hello, Ms. Parker, it's Marcel Bishop. I'm calling personally to congratulate you" he said.

"I got the job?" Trinity asked, striving to conceal her exhilaration.

"Yes. When would you like to begin your training?" he asked.

"I can start right away if you like" Trinity said.

"Alright, contact my assistant Aria tomorrow to get your schedule."

"Thank you Mr. Bishop, you won't be sorry."

"Call me Marcel," he said.

"Ok, well, thank you again, Marcel." Trinity said and she hung up the phone, then began to dial Lisa to tell her the good news, when it suddenly rang.

"Hey girl, what cha doing?" Lisa asked.

"Hi Lisa, I was just about to call you."

"I got the position!"

"Marcellus just hung up, and oh, he told me to call him Marcel." Trinity said to her friend.

"Don't you think that sounds a little too forward?" Lisa asked Trinity.

"After all, you really don't know much about each other for you to shorten his name like that," Lisa stated.

"Call the man whatever he wants you to call him. He just gave you a chance of a lifetime, and who knows, you may get something else out of it." Lisa said.

"Don't say that. Lisa, unlike you and Sara, you know I don't date anyone I work with, and besides, I have Colin."

"Yeah, what a treat." "Trin, we have to find you someone else, Colin just doesn't do it for me."

"Wait, I thought he was my boyfriend, Lisa."

"Hahaha, if you say so."

"Alright, enough of Colin for now," Trinity said.

"Lets go pick Sara up and celebrate my new found wealth."

"Sounds like a plan. We can meet at my apartment."

"Ok, see you in a bit." Trinity said.

Marcel knew that he made the right decision in giving Trinity the manager's position at his restaurant. He was a sharp judge of character and had been watching how she handled the assistant manager's job. He thought to himself, Trinity is highly liked by all of the staff. Her presence alone soothes and eases them. Her training will be stringent, but she can handle it.

"The way I feel about her, she can probably handle me as well." Marcel said to himself.

"I'll wait a few days to make sure she is comfortable in the job then I'll make my move." I think she likes me well enough. I've noticed how she eyes me when she thinks I'm not paying attention," he continued to say.

"Ahh, the things I'd like to do to her body."

Marcel felt himself getting rock hard just thinking about spreading her out on his bed, wrapping his arms around her, sucking on her breasts, tasting her, having her submit, then filling her cunt full with his cock.

"At least I can offer her more than that so-called boyfriend of hers can."

"What's his name?" Oh yeah, Colin. Shady guy. I don't trust him. I don't like the way he looks at her. He looks as though he wants to make her hurt, and not in a good way."

"Why am I wasting my time thinking about Colin?" Marcel thought.

"I need a shower, some liquid and some sleep; not necessarily in that order."

"I'll see to things later tonight from the restaurant."

The Fabulous Three, as they call themselves, were out on the town and ready to party. They had been bar-hopping for the last two hours, drinking, dancing, laughing and having a good time. While sitting at the bar waiting for the next round of drinks to arrive, Trin turned around to survey the bar and noticed a tall dark stranger standing near the door. She gasped, and her friends turned towards her to ask what was wrong. She turned to answer them then turned back to where the stranger was standing.

"He's gone."

"What?" Lisa probed.

"He's gone."

"Who's gone Trinity?"

"Have you had too much to drink, already?" Lisa asked, smirking as she touched Trinity's arm."

They're looking at me as if I've gone mad, Trinity thought.

Trinity began to recall the dream she had been having virtually every night and there was always a tall dark stranger. She never saw his face. Like just now, she thought. He wasn't even five feet away, yet I didn't see his face. She decided—against her better judgment— to tell her friends about her dreams.

"You need to stay with us for the weekend and have Simon pick Scott up for a sleepover. We'll see to it that you're ok. No one will get to you with the three of us together," Lisa pleaded, as she softly caressed Trinity's hand.

Trinity hesitated, her eyes searching the shadowy bar for the stranger, and then answered.

"It's Wednesday ladies, remember?"

"I start training tomorrow."

"So, just make the call. You're staying here, in the city." Lisa said to Trinity.

"Okay!"

"You said Colin was in your dream, right?" Sara said.

"Yes." Trinity answered.

"What was he doing?"

"Did he help you?" Lisa asked.

"No, he ran." Trinity said.

Almost simultaneously, Lisa and Sara blurted, "What a chicken shit prick." The three of them burst into laughter. They paid for their final round of drinks. Trinity phoned Simon and asked him to see to Scott. Afterwards, the three ladies strolled out of the bar towards their apartment building.

Just across the street, hidden in an ominous alleyway, stood the tall dark stranger; waiting, watching, following.

"She'll be safe tonight." the stranger said.

"I'll see to it."

"No one will harm her."

"No one will touch her."

"She belongs to me." *MINE*

It was the middle of the night and Trinity was sleeping over at Sara's. She started to toss and turn. The recurrent dream was terrorizing her. As always, it starts with Colin running. He was always running, but from what and why, she had no clue. However, there was something different about the dream this time. There was a disturbing noise, and the fierce odor of chemicals. Out of nowhere, she hears screaming and ear-piercing shots in the dark. Behind her, flames appear, preventing her from escaping the way she came. She's trapped. As she shouts at the top of her lungs for Colin, he steps from behind a half-closed door. He starts coming toward her with something in his hands. Then the tall dark stranger appears. His face is unseen. His voice is resonant and commanding as he says, "Come to me, Trinity. Come to me, now. I am here to protect you. I won't let him hurt you." Her eyes grow wide with horror, as Colin advances on her. Unexpectedly, the stranger steps in front of her and shields her from whatever Colin is about to do to her. A fight ensues, she screams, tossing the covers from her legs. She tries to run. She awakes just before she hits the floor.

Sara ran into her room only to find her sprawled out across the bed. Trinity's face looked as though she has just watched a very frightening scene from a horror movie. She told Sara about the dream in an attempt to regain some composure. Embracing her friend protectively, Sara said, "Let's go to the kitchen and have a cup of warm milk."

"My mom always gave me a cup of warm milk before bed," Trinity said, struggling to keep the tears in. "She said it would help me sleep through the night. I really miss mom and dad, but especially mom and some of the talks we used to have.

"Hey kiddo, you can always talk to Lisa and me."

"Thanks Sara."

"Anytime. Now, let's hit the sack. You don't want to be late for your first day of training do you? And after work on Thursday, we can hang out."

"That sounds good to me. I'll call you when I have free time to let you know the time and place to meet up."

"Now sleep, I'm tired." Trinity yawned.

Trin headed back to bed, but couldn't get back to sleep, so she decided to take a shower. She heard a knock in the distance and thought; Sara can't get back to sleep. She must want to talk. "Come in" Trinity yelled. "I'll be out in a minute." Just as she finished drying off and started heading towards the bedroom, she heard something. She called out, but no one answered.

She shrugged her shoulders and headed to the bedroom only to find the mysterious tall dark stranger standing there.

"Who are you?"

"What do you want?" she asked, overcome with a strange sense of inquisitiveness. He stood there still in the shadows of the room, and said nothing. She asked again, "Who are you and how did you get in here?" "I climbed up the fire escape and entered through the window after I heard you say come in," he said, as he slowly walked towards her. "I guess you thought I was your friend, the one who is sleeping in the other room. You should be more careful about leaving your window open, anyone can come in." As he said that, she began to back away swiftly, but calmly. "Tell me why you're here or I'll scream," she said. "You should have done that when you first noticed me, but since you didn't. You won't now." "Don't be so sure. My friend will come running if I scream."

"You won't scream because you want me here. I know you want me here, said the stranger. You dream of me. I've been in your dreams for some time and each time your dream is different, but I'm in it." "How do you know what my dreams are about?" Trinity asked. "I don't even understand them. "Wait, I saw you tonight." At the bar, she stated. "I was with my girlfriends, and you were near the door. Then you were gone."

"Yes, I was and now I am here." "You followed me?"

"Yes, I'm here to protect you, to keep you safe. You need my help."

"Excuse me. What the hell are you talking about? You don't even know me or anything about me, and I certainly don't know you. And I don't need your help with anything."

"I know all about you and your family Trinity, and you do need my help." The stranger continued.

"Do you have a name?"

"Yes." He answered.

"Do you want to tell me what it is?"

"No, not yet." "I want to look at you. You are beautiful, Trinity. The most perfect woman I've ever seen." "Oh great, you know my name, but I can't know yours and you think I'm perfect for you. What a crock.

"Get out!"

"Just let me look at you."

"I have a boyfriend." "Colin? I've seen him, no big deal. He's a wimp and acts like one as well."

"How would you know?"

"I've seen the two of you together. You don't mesh. Furthermore, he can't protect you. From the looks of him, he probably won't if there's trouble."

"Get out of my room!"

"I want you Trinity, and I will have you."

"Listen, whoever you are you're crazy if you think that I'm going to do anything for you or with you."

"Come to me, Trinity. I want you. I've wanted you since the moment I saw you."

"When was that exactly?" I first saw you in Rhode Island. Then at home with your parents, and finally when you moved here, in the city.

I lost track of you for a while, you stopped dreaming, but only for a short while. It was during the time of your move to NY. You started dreaming again and I found you. You began working at the Palace the first night I saw you in the city, and though I couldn't reach out to you, I decided to keep a close watch over you. The night you moved into this building, I watched over you and when your parents left, I felt an even stronger need to protect you. I have been coming here every night since then, to make sure you were safe. I watch over you at your home now."

"You know where I live? You follow me all around?"

"Yes, but only at night, someone else takes over for me during the day. Your dreams are a warning that something bad is about to happen and you should heed that warning."

Her mouth fell open at what he was telling her. Trin began to feel overwhelmed, as the stranger stepped further into the dimly lit room. "Please, don't come any closer," she said. "I won't hurt you," he replied, in a deep raspy voice. A gasp slipped from her mouth as she focused on his eyes. They are so obscure they almost look black with a little fleck of red in the center. His long dark-colored shoulder length hair was slightly covering his face. He had the most beautiful set of lips she'd ever seen on a man. A stone chiseled face, broad shoulders and the outline of his body revealed a massive chest under his tight shirt. The look of his strong sturdy thighs and the bulge at the center of his black jeans pushing out his zipper was huge. He reminded her of someone else, but who?

She thought to herself, I need to get away from this man and, scream for help, anything. Realizing she isn't moving, he came even closer. She licked her lips and took a deep breath, before she could say anything, he was on her. He pressed his lips to her mouth, sucked on her lower lip asking for permission to enter. Trinity held her lips tightly together as she felt his tongue trying to part them. She finally parted her lips and he kissed her hard, sucking on her tongue, darting it in and out of her mouth. Their tongues circled each other, she felt something pointy in his mouth when her tongue darted in. She broke the kiss and pulled back to look into his eyes, but couldn't begin to explain what she saw there. She thought she must be mad, or in some alternate universe, because all she could think about right now was his touch. Trinity placed her lips back on his again and heard him groan.

Without breaking the kiss, he lifted her in his arms, and placed her gently in the middle of the bed. He took the towel that she used to dry herself with and pulled it tighter around her, and kissed her harder. He broke the kiss long enough to say,

"Julian."

"What?" she asked, perplexed.

"My name, it's Julian."

"What will you do to me?" He stopped for a minute to think about how to answer that question. He wanted to mark her as his, but couldn't, not yet.

"I want to hold you Trinity."

"I want to touch you in ways you've never been touched before."

Trinity whimpered as his hand gripped the back of her neck. Julian covered her mouth with his, kissing her gently at first, then passionately. A moan escaped her and she felt heat welling up from between her thighs. He licked a trail down her neck and covered her breasts with his big hands.

He teased her nipples until they turned into hard pebbles. Another moan and she asked him to touch her more. As she glided a leg up and down his thigh, she could feel his cock stiffen even more.

"I must be insane for letting this happen, she thought, but I can't seem to stop myself. I want this. I want him."

She could feel a rush of emotion building within her. Their lips separated and he licked down her body, drawing a nipple into his mouth and sucking it hard. She whispered, "Harder, please." Julian stopped long enough to take the other nipple in his mouth to give it the same attention.

"Julian, take me," as she squeezed her eyes shut, waiting to feel him. "Julian, please, I'm holding on as though I'm on a cliff and I am about to fall off." He smiled and kissed his way down her legs to that sweet little spot between her thighs.
"Please take me," she begged.

"No."

"Please," she insisted.

"Be patient."

"How?" I want you to take me. "Please."

"Not yet."

He spread Trinity's legs wider and licked up her slit, feeling the hard little nub. She wiggled, no longer able to hold still. He slid a finger in and worked it around, as she worked herself on his hands. He slid another finger in touching her G-spot. "Please" she said again. "I can't take much more of this." Finally, he stared into her eyes and said, "Let go Trinity. Let go, now." She exploded as her orgasm overwhelmed her so much she started shaking. Julian slid up beside her to hold her and she shook in his arms. She reached out to touch him as he took her mouth and kissed her hard. She wanted more of what he had to offer. She wanted to feel him inside her. He started something that needed to be finished. What she felt with Colin just didn't compare to what Julian was doing to her.

Again, she begged, "Please, touch me Julian." Again, his answer was no. He couldn't tell her why. Julian knew if he told her what he was, she would either not believe him or go into shock and never forgive herself for being with him.

She grabbed him to pull him into her. "No, I don't want to hurt you. I might be too big for you."

"But, I want to feel you inside me. Take me, please Julian take me." Trinity leaded.

He reared back then let out a loud roar, which frightened her.

"I have to leave Trinity. I have to leave now."

"Why?" I want you to stay. I want to feel more of you."

"I know and I want to give you more, but I don't have enough time right now," Julian said.

"I will always be around if you need me."

As Julian stood up to leave, Trinity said, "The next time you feel the need to come protect me, come to my front door." Julian smiled, kissed her once more then left through the window.

Chapter 3

Somewhere in the suburbs of Rhode Island, a meeting was taking place in the shadows between Giles Butler, Charlie Anson and Bill Hogate; they were all friends and business partners of James Parker.

"We're all here, Giles," said Charlie.

"When are we going to move on this thing? Time is running out on the plans that we made regarding that Parker girl," Charlie stated.

"I was looking forward to taking over when James retired. Charlie said; but now, there's nothing for any of us, and what's worse is he left things to that twit of a daughter."

"Look, I have a few things going in that department, which should be coming to fruition, very soon," said Giles.

"Is he in place?"

"Yes, and I also have a backup if he fails."

"Wait a minute," Bill said.

"Who is he?"

"Colin." Giles said.

"You've got to be kidding!" Bills said.

"No, I'm not, Bill."

"I gave Colin this assignment and he will carry it out."

"Or what, Giles?

"He's your own son!"

"Yes, but Trinity doesn't know that."

.   "She doesn't know I have a son. She hasn't made the association because the last names are different."

"Yeah, but damn, own your son? Why get family involved in this when we can easily do the deed ourselves." Bill exclaimed.

"I'll do it, after all, I was the one who tampered with James's plane," Bill added.

"Yes, well, we will meet back here again in two weeks with everything finalized," Giles said.

"Now if you will excuse me gentlemen, I have a plane to catch back to New York."

Trin was preparing for work, but decided to call home and speak with her brothers, just to check in. Simon told her to stay in the city with her friends for the weekend. Alex and him would be at the house for Scott and would see to feeding him. He needed a male figure around him right now. She felt guilty about not being home with Scott, but understood and wished she could help him. She also knew he needed to be around his big brother more often.

The night shift was busy on a Friday night. Everybody seemed to be coming in from a play, movie or just having a night out on the town. The place was packed to the rafters, and there was a line of patrons waiting to be seated. Live entertainment on the weekends made it all the more appealing. The bar was crowded, the tables were full, even the booths upstairs were all occupied and the wait staff was bustling. Everything seemed to be at a hurried pace and Trinity was in charge of it all.

Trinity loved her new position.   She hadn't seen the owner of the restaurant yet, but the night was still young. Marcel could waltz in at any time.

Colin came in, sitting in his favorite seat at the bar, studying her as she strolled out to mingle with a few of the guests and stars that were there. Trinity stopped over to see him. She wanted to tell him she would be with the girls this weekend and maybe they could spend some time together.

"Sure," he said with a seedy look on his face.

"What's wrong?" Trinity asked. Just as he was about to answer her, she froze. Trinity knew the minute Julian walked through the door.

She turned in time to notice Julian going upstairs to one of the booths. He was dressed in a black tux with crisp white shirt and bowtie that fit him perfectly. He looks too beautiful to be a man if you can even call a man beautiful, she thought. When she returned her gaze to Colin, his eyes had hardened; they had been following who she was looking at. Her face tinted with a light blush when Colin asked her who that was. Trinity didn't lie when she said, "I don't know. This is the first time I've ever seen him here."

She faced Colin, who was still sitting with his back to the bar. She knew that behind that curtain, Julian could see as she continued to speak with Colin. He was staring straight at her. She could feel the heat on her back from his eyes.

"Can I come over tonight after you close up? I want to spend some time with you."

Trinity thought better about saying no. She wanted Julian with her tonight, but gave in and said yes to Colin.

"I'm leaving now, Colin voiced, but I will be back to pick you up at 3:00am."

"Ok?" he asked.

"Ok," Trinity replied, and he gave her a quick peck on the lips then headed for the exit.

She thought she heard a growl coming from upstairs. She looked around, but saw nothing. As she headed back to the office, Marcel made his appearance with his assistant Aria. After saying his hi's and hello's to those he knew, he approached Trinity to greet her and ask how things were going. He could see for himself that all was well. He just wanted to be near her. Trinity answered Marcel's questions, then stepped back and took an elongated look at him. Marcel was very tall, with dark hair, dark eyes, and was built almost the same way as Julian. On top of that, he spoke with a related familiarity, he was also in a black tux and he too looked gorgeous. Apparently, he had been at the same gathering as most of the people there.

Marcel stared back at Trin then asked, "Is there anything wrong?"

"Do you have a brother?" she asked.

He looked at her as though she drove a stake through his heart. He didn't want to answer her, but knew he had to. The only reason she would have asked this question was if she had met Julian and if that happened to be the case, his brother has already taken her from him before he could stake a claim on her himself.

Marcel thought, he must also be protecting her from something or someone. Whenever he showed up, someone was in trouble or in need of his assistance. He especially likes to help damsels in distress but doesn't get close to them.

Does she know who we are he wonder? Maybe not or she would have said so by now.

"I need to find my brother." Marcel quietly thought to himself.

"Yes, Trinity, I have a brother. His name is Julian. Have you met him?"

"Um," she said timidly, "yes, I did last night."

"And may I ask where?"

"I found him in my room when I came out of the shower." Trinity stated.

"How did he get in?"

"He said he climbed the fire escape and came in through the window. I heard what I thought was a knock at my door by my roommate and invited her in, only to find him instead."

Well, Marcel thought, she doesn't know who he is and he hasn't staked a claim on her. He would need her permission to do that.

"I will have a talk with Julian, and tell him to stay away from you if that is what you wish."

"No! Marcel, I can handle my own affairs. Thank you though. I think I can handle Julian."

"However, if you want to talk to him, he's upstairs in booth 4."

Marcel digested that bit of news and headed upstairs to see his brother. He needed to find out what was happening with his new manager and if he had a chance with her.

****

Colin left the Palace in a hurry. He had to get this new info to his father fast and see what steps he needed to take now. He drove out to his father's house, in the suburbs of New York, and was let in by Chadwick, his father's bodyguard.

He went straight to his father's study.
"Hello, son. How are you this evening?" his father said, reclined in his office chair."

"Fine dad. Look, I have some news."

"Oh."

"Yes, about Trinity."

Giles Butler stopped reading the New York Times and looked up at his son with interest.

"What is it?"

"She's seeing someone else."

"How do you know that, Colin?"

"I was with her at the Palace tonight when this man walked in and went upstairs."

"Annnd?"

"They looked at each other as though they were lovers."

"Did he speak to her, son?"

"No, just nodded and went into a booth, but the stares they gave each other were so...."

"So what, son?"

"I don't know dad."

"Trinity said she would be spending the weekend in the city with her friends, so I asked if I could spend the night with her."

"Colin, where is this going?" Giles asked.

"She hesitated, dad."

"She has never done that."

"I see."

"Are you jealous?"

"Do you have feelings for her now?"

"No dad."

"Good, because in the end, those feelings won't mean a damn thing." Giles said.

"She has to go."

"So, are you staying with her tonight?" "Yes, I have to pick her up at 3:00am."

"That's good to know because we need time to make our plans." After going over the fine details of their secret plans concerning Trinity Parker, Colin and Giles concluded their meeting.

"Everything has to be in place within the next two weeks," Giles said, and after that, we make our move. There will be no going back, Colin."

"I understand dad."

"See that you do." "Now, it's time for you to head back to the city and pick up your assignment."

****

Marcel left Aria downstairs to mingle with friends while he went to talk to his brother. He entered booth #4 and saw Julian just sitting there looking down at the woman who would be his.

"Hello, brother." Marcel bellowed.

"What are you up to these days?" he said to Julian.

"Hey Bro, not much." Julian answered.

"What's up?"

"Oh I think you know, Julian." Marcel said with a look on his face that said you better tell me everything.

"I want to know why."

"Why what" "What are we talking about here, Marcel.

"Why do you feel that you have to be protective of her?"

"Protect who." Julian said with a smirk on his face. He knew to what his brother was referring.

"I'm asking you again brother, what are you talking about."

"Don't play dumb with me Julian. I know you, and you wouldn't be here if you weren't protecting someone."

"Ok." "Ok." You win, I give up, Julian said.

"I can't get into specifics right now, but I'm going to need your help on this one."

"Anything you need you know you got it." Marcel said.

"Julian, I need to ask you something and I don't want you to take it the wrong way."

"What is it?"

"Have you claimed Trinity as your mate?"

"No, not yet but I plan to."

"Why? Are you interested in her Marcel?"

"Yes, and I have been since I first laid eyes on her."

"So have I, brother." Julian stated. "So don't even think about it Marcel."

"Look, she has been here with me for a few years now and had no idea she needed protection."

Marcel lost some of his ability to sense things after the last time he went out on a detail, and was almost killed. He didn't sense a needing of protection from Trinity.

"I have seen her with her boyfriend, Marcel said, and I don't like it."

"Something is definitely wrong with him. I just can't put my finger on it."

"I know what you mean, Mar." Julian said calling his brother by his nickname.

"I've been watching him, too, and whatever he's involved in, has to do with Trinity."

"She needs us, both of us. Just... don't touch her Mar."

"You just want to fuck her, Jules."

"No, it's more than that, I want to possess her."

"Fine." Marcel said.

"I'm leaving anyway to take Aria home, but I'll be back."

"Let's go hunting for donors together the way we used to do back home Jules."

"Sure, why not, it might even be fun." Julian stated.

****

Colin returned just before the doors were closed and locked for the night. Trinity came out of the office and fixed him a drink, then looked around to see what needed to be done before leaving for the night. The restaurant was spotless. On her way out, the staff bid her a good night.

Trinity and Colin headed over to Sara's apartment. Once inside, they made their way to the spare bedroom. Trinity started to undress so she could take a hot shower, but was stopped by Colin.

"What are you doing?" Colin asked.

"I need to take a shower," Trinity answered, more irritated than curious.

"Your shower can wait. I want to fuck you, now," he spat, as he began to pull her down on the bed. She tried to stop him, but he started ripping off her clothes.

"No, Colin."

"Why not?" You never had a problem with me before. What's different now, Trinity?"

"You're being rough with me is what's different."

"Are you sleeping with one of those brothers?"

"No!" Look, there is no one else, Colin. I've never cheated on you." "Can you say the same to me?" she asks, despising the imprudent smirk on his face. He was silent.

"I thought not, you haven't treated me like a girlfriend at all lately."

"We have fast sex and you rush off, telling me you have to get up early for a meeting or you have to go out of town." I feel like a piece of meat to you Colin."

Colin's smirk grew wider as he stepped over to Trinity. "I'm sorry you feel that way Trinity." The last thing I want to do is have you angry with me all night."

"Lets go to bed, I can't hold this much longer, Trinity. I need relief now baby." Colin said.

"Get off me and get out!"

"Trinity, come on, just a little, I promise I'll make it good for you." At the top of her

lungs, she screamed."

"Get the hell out, NOW!!"

The bedroom door opened with a loud bang, Sara was standing there with a broom in her hands, pointing the way to the front door.

"Leave my apartment Colin and don't come back or I'll call the police."

He rose up to leave then turned around, he looked between Trinity and Sara and back to Trinity and said, "You bitch, you'll be sorry."

"You think you're so special, well, we'll see just how special you are."

"You're gonna get yours and soon." Colin said.

"Get out Colin." Sara said again.

Colin headed for the door, turned around and looked back at Trinity once more, smirked and then left.

****

Julian was standing across the street from the apartment building in the shadows with his brother. They heard the whole conversation from where they stood. They waited for Colin to exit the building and head for his car before they made their move. That night, Colin became an unwilling donor. He was quickly whisked away by the brothers and almost drained dry. They reluctantly left him alive because they wanted to find out what he was up to, as far as Trinity was concerned.

Chapter 4

Sara sat with her friend until she calmed down. "Let me make you a hot cup of tea or warm milk or how about a drink to calm your nerves." "No thanks to the drink, I'll take the warm milk. You go back to bed, I can get it." "Alright, yell if you need me."

"Thanks Sara, I will."

Trin heard a scratch at the door and peeked through the peephole before she opened it. "What are you doing here?" she asked. "I could sense you needed me, so here I am," he said. "Come in Julian and thanks for using the front door this time." They both laugh and headed to the kitchen.

"I'm making a cup of hot milk it helps me to get to sleep." Trinity said.

"Leave the milk. I'll help you get to sleep." Julian said.

"What?"

"How?"

"Never mind."

"Let's go to your bedroom."

"You go; I'll be there in a minute." Trinity said to Julian.

"It's down the hall, third door on the left. Sara is in the first room, so please be quiet."

"Come with me," he says and leads her to the bedroom. "Lie down and let me hold you. You can go to sleep in my arms."

Trinity rested there, safe in his arms, wondering, what is it about this man that makes me want to do as he asks.

Julian knew he only has a few hours left before daylight, but doesn't care, as long as he is with her. She turned her head to face him and placed the softest kiss on his lips. He took that as a sign she wanted to do more than be held and he was right. She moved closer to him, while sliding her hands under his shirt, and began to play with the flat nubs on his chest. He let out a moan and stopped her before she could get her hands any further down his body.

"Are you sure you want to do this with me? Because once I enter your body Trinity, you will belong to me and only me, but before I take you, I have to tell you or better yet, show you something. After this, you may not want to have anything to do with me. You may even alert the authorities to have my brother and me taken away."

"What does this have to do with your brother?" she asked, puzzled.

"Just tell me the truth Julian. Don't make me wait any longer. I've been through a lot in my life. I think I can handle whatever it is you have to say."

"Alright Trinity, alright."

Knowing he was about to put everything on the line for the sake of the love of the woman he wanted, Julian faced her, his eyes started to change colors. They went from brown to completely black and then the eyeballs disappeared altogether, being replaced by a red glow. Trinity began sliding up out of bed to move to the door, but is halted when she realized she couldn't get her feet to go. Julian opened his mouth to reveal a set of fangs.

"You know, I've read about this stuff in books, but I've never seen anything like this in real life. What the hell am I saying? Why me? Why is this shit happening to me?" she asked, then the lights went out.

Trinity was awakened by a tender kiss. She looked up and saw Julian staring into her eyes.

"Am I going mad? Did I just have another bad dream with a monster in it this time?"

"No," Julian said. You're not going mad and you didn't have a nightmare. You are right about one thing though, in the eyes of most I am considered a monster.

"Are you afraid of me now, Trinity?

"No." I'm not afraid Julian but I need to hear from your own lips what I already know.

"Vampire," he said, I'm a vampire."

"Somewhere in the back of my mind, I knew there was something different about you. The way you spoke and acted, the way I felt the first night you were here; as though there was something between us, which had not yet been spoken.

Somehow, I'm supposed to be with you, although I don't know how that could be. We don't know each other on that kind of level."

"I should leave."

"Please, stay Julian. I want you to stay."

"Why?"

"Tell me why, Trinity."

"I'm not afraid of you."

"I think of you constantly, even when I'm in a state of rest. I've fallen in love with you, Trinity. My love for you grows even stronger with each passing second. We are meant to be together, always."

"Julian, I need to ask you some questions. Will you answer them?" "Yes, I have no reason to lie to you. Ask me what you want to know." "Will our being together change anything about me? What I'm asking is will I become a vampire?" "No, Trinity, it takes a lot more than us having sex for you to become like me. And in answer to your thoughts, no, I can't give you any diseases. "How did you know I was......never mind?" Julian chuckled at that.

"There is something else that you should know." "What is it?" "My brother, he has feelings for you too, and if he is the one you want to be with, I won't interfere. But, just know that no matter what I will protect you, always." "I like your brother, but not in the way you think. We have an employer employee relationship. You are the man I want to be with."

"I'm not a man, Trinity. I'm a monster and if you wish, you can kill me now with silver." "You're not a monster Julian, and I don't want to kill you. I want to be with you." "Would you do something for me then? Call me Jules. That's the name I've gone by since I was small. Father is the only one who still calls me Julian." "I will call you Jules if you call me Trin." "I would baby, but frankly, I rather like calling you by your given name because no one else does." "Well, I like calling you by your given name, too. So now that's settled, kiss me, Julian!!" "With much pleasure my lady!"

Julian began kissing her, he could hear her heart beating wildly and sense the call of her blood as he trailed kisses down her neck, and it frightened him. He didn't want to hurt her, he wanted to make love to her and mark her so that everyone would know that she was his. He licked down her stomach and stuck his tongue in her navel, then licked his way down to her v. She was clean shaven and smelled of lilacs. Her legs parted and he delved right in, eager to taste her. After a few more teasing licks, he latched onto her clit and sucked hard. Licking and sucking until her body arched off the bed as waves of pleasure hit her nerves. She was holding onto the crumpled sheets, ready to burst. Her orgasm came on fast and rocked her to her core. Julian raised a hand to stifle her moans in order to keep her friend from running into the room.

He slid up her body and kissed her fiercely with a thirst that only she could quench, wanting to bite her and make her his. He thought, I have to wait. My bite is forbidden unless she gives me permission to do so. He could see the veins in her exposed neck, summoning him to taste her.

"Take me Jules please. I want to feel you inside me," she begged. He rose up on both arms and positioned himself between her legs. She was exceedingly wet and ready for him. He played at her entrance with the head of his cock, while Trinity moaned and wiggled her tight little ass around. Then, without warning, he thrust half way into her and pulled back leaving the head in. "Do that again," she commanded him. He thrust the entire length of himself into her in one stroke. "OH MY GAWD," she said, feeling as though she was going to split in two. Julian was balls deep inside her, fucking with all he had and then some. She was matching him, thrust for thrust; the tension was building in both of them. His balls were tightening; he held her thighs in place as he pumped into her; he wasn't going to be able to hold out much longer and the taste for blood, her blood was getting stronger.

She wrapped her legs around his waist. He could feel her walls tighten around his cock. While arching her back, Trinity felt the urge to tell Julian to bite her. She had no idea where that came from. She dug into his ass with her nails, pushed her pussy forward and screamed his name as her orgasm shot through her. Julian, still pumping followed her over, filling her with his seed; marking her as his. **MINE!!**

She milked him dry and yet he still wanted more. She was spent, fully sated. She kissed his soft lips. Their tongues darting in and out and circling each other, she was becoming aroused again. Julian didn't release her, his dick was semi-hard and still in her sheath. Julian knew that he should leave before it was too late. Her veins looked so inviting and he was thirsty. Instead, he stayed. He couldn't leave her, his Trinity.

Julian lowered his head and began licking around her nipple then sucking, while she moaned and pushed her breasts forward to give him better access. He gave both nipples equal attention licking and sucking, feeling them grow hard in his mouth. Julian's dick became fully hard while he was inside her. He started moving slow at first then picked up speed, rocking into her with a force so strong he felt that he just couldn't get enough of her. She was fucking him back with the same equal force and passion. Their hearts were beating so fast he could hear hers; he could hear the blood flowing through her veins. His fangs started to extend. Julian turned his head so she couldn't see them, knowing how badly he wanted to taste her. He had to stop, he didn't want to hurt her but he just couldn't bring himself to stop. She felt so good beneath him. His cock was throbbing ready to explode. He wanted them to cum together.

She was on fire, lost to her emotions; his touch, his taste and his musky smell were enough to set any woman on fire but she was the one under him, feeling him push her to the limit with his hard steady grind.

You are driving me crazy, I can't hold this much longer. "Then let go baby, come for me." Wrap your legs around me and let go. Let me feel you strangle my cock in your pussy. I can't hold out too much longer either. Come for me Trinity, come now. Her orgasm shot through her so fast at that command, she couldn't keep her mouth shut, and Julian was no better, they came together. His growling woke Sara but she didn't come into the room.

Sara called my name only once. She must have thought I was dreaming and went back to sleep, Trinity thought. After they calmed down from round two of their earth-shattering lovemaking, they stretched out on the bed and held each other until almost dawn.

"I have to leave you now baby, but I'll be back tonight. If you don't see me right away, wait for me. We can come back here together. Don't leave without me Trinity. I want you safe," he said. They embraced once more before he left. He kissed Trinity gently before breaking apart and stared into her eyes, tilted her head back, and kissed her again with such an overpowering force, it almost knocked her off her feet.

I love you Trinity!

Julian released Trinity from his embrace, and just before the sun began to rise above the treetops, Julian was gone. She sat in the middle of the bed just looking over at the window, watching the sun come up and hoping that Julian made it safely to his destination. A stream of tears began to trickle down her face. She was falling in love with him, too.

****

Colin woke up in the alleyway across from the girls' apartment building feeling like he had been drugged. He managed to get to his car before he passed out again. By the time he awoke, he was struggling to figure out what had happened to him and why he was feeling so out of it. One thing he did know; he was going to find out what that bitch was up to in case he had to make his move sooner than planned.

In the meantime, Trin visited the law firm of Winslow and Campbell with the intention of having the firm represent her and take control of disposing all of her holdings with the Textile Company.

Scott and Simon were already financially taken care of. Scott would come into his money when he was twenty-one, and Simon had invested wisely in his high end furniture store. The balance of his inheritance, he was putting to good use. She knew Simon and Alex planned to get married one day and have kids. Scott would be going off to college once he graduated high school, but would still need somewhere to call home; especially, when he came to visit during breaks and holidays. In light of that, all three of them decided to keep the house for Scott and she could eventually move back into the city.

****

The dream began with Trin calling out for help and running through a warehouse. There was that chemical smell again. It was the same odor as in her other dreams. She ran until she noticed some barrels and hid behind them, ducking whoever was after her. She heard footsteps, then voices. Someone called Colin's name. She peeked around the barrels and noticed Colin standing in the middle of the floor with a knife in his hand. The look on his face was maniacal.

I need to get out of here, she thought, and stepped out into the open to run. Before she could take off, Julian was suddenly there shielding her. "Stay here," he said. "I'll get you out." She looked up just in time to see Colin coming toward Julian with the knife raised in his right hand. Her scream woke her and she sat straight up in the bed just as Sara entered her room. "Are you still having that same dream?" Sara asked. "Yeah and it's beginning to get worse." "I'll make an appointment for you with Dr. Marshall. You need to be seen right away." She was still shaking like a leaf, when Sara gave her a slip of paper with a date and time on it. "Here, I just made the appointment. You are to see the doctor at 5:00pm this evening. I'll let Marcel know that you'll be in later. I called Lisa and she is going with you. We can talk about everything later. Get yourself ready and I'll see you tonight." "Thanks Sara." "Hey girl, what are friends for?"

****

Although he was in a state of rest, he saw her dream. He also knew there was a connection between Giles and Colin, but what? Julian needed to be with the woman he loved, but had to wait until sundown before he could go out. He raised at twilight, was showered, dressed and headed out the door. He was on a mission, he had to see his woman. He needed to hold her, and make sure she was okay.

****

"Good evening Trinity, come in. You're right on time," Dr. Marshall said. "Hello, doctor," she replied. "Have a seat and we can talk about what's going on with you." Once seated, she began to explain her dreams in detail to the doctor. When she finished talking, Dr. Marshall took notes and made several suggestions that would help her to sleep and hopefully derail the bad dreams she was having. "Before I suggest any medication, let me examine you."

Upon completion of her exam, Dr. Marshall gave her a mild sedative. "This will not interfere with any other medications you might be taking. It will help you to sleep through the night, but in the event you continue to have this problem, I can prescribe something a tad bit stronger. On your way out, make an appointment with my secretary for three weeks from today. I want to follow-up with you." "Okay doctor, thank you." She made her new appointment and left.

"Thanks for coming with me Lisa. Trinity said. I didn't think I would need support, but I sure am glad you were here." "Stop that. We're friends. Sara and I will always be here for you girl. Now we better get to work. I'll drive. We're late, only by an hour though. Marcel is covering until we get there."

It was busy for a Thursday night. The bar was full and people were on the dance floor. There were several celebrations taking place in different areas of the restaurant. After Trinity checked in with Marcel, she returned to the floor to check on staff and nod at the guests. She noticed Colin when he came in. Instead of going to the bar, he marched straight for her

She thought, I don't have the energy to deal with him right now. He just doesn't get it. Why can't he just leave me alone? This is so exasperating and seeing him isn't helping things much. "I need to talk to you Trinity," he said. "Why Colin?" she asked, impatiently. "I want to apologize for last night and I have a few other things I want to say."

"Colin, we don't have anything else to say to each other, we are finished." Trinity said.

"Look at me, Trin. Look at me when you tell me that."

"That's not necessary; this conversation isn't necessary. Just get away from me."

He grabbed her arm and demanded that she look at him. When his voice raised an octave some of the staff took notice. Jade ran to the office and came back with Marcel.

"Is everything ok out here?" Marcel asked coldly, his eyes dark and menacing and glued to Colin.

Marcel noticed the tight grip Colin had on Trinity.

"Let her go." It became a staring contest between Marcel and Colin. They glowered at each other until whatever it was he saw in Marcel's eyes, caused him to back away, but his hand was still clamped down on her arm, Marcel stepped closer to Colin.

"I'm not going to tell you again, so you'd better do it, now," Marcel sneered.

Colin released her arm, but not before squeezing it as tight as he could and pushing her into Marcel.

"You are such a bitch. You crossed the wrong person. Mark my words, you will pay for this." Colin said hatefully, malice in every word.

"Are you all right?" Marcel asked.

"Yes, thanks for coming to my rescue, Marcel. And thank you too Jade," Trinity said.

Just then, Julian walked in and noticed the looks on everyone's faces as he rushed to Trinity's side.

"What's wrong?"

"Colin was here and laid hands on her," Marcel said. "Jade came into the office to get me and when I walked out to the floor, he was putting the squeeze on her arm. He just left," Marcel explained.

"Look, guys, I'm fine. I'll have a bruise later, but other than that, I'm okay," Trinity said, not believing her own words. She was shaken by the incident.

Julian brushed a lock of her hair back behind her ear and said, "Stay here with my brother. I'll be right back." "No, Julian. Let it go. Please," she beseeched. He looked to his brother. They nodded to each other. "We'll be upstairs if you need anything. When we come back down, I'm taking you home. Marcel can handle the rest of the shift tonight or one of your friends can fill in for you."

The brothers were upstairs for the better part of an hour. When they came back down to the main floor, Marcel spoke with Jade and asked her to finish Trinity's shift

"Marcel told me Jade is going to finish my shift," Trinity said to Julian. She leaned in close to him and whispered, "you'll have me all to yourself. My friends won't be home for three more hours, at least." That was more than enough time for them to do major damage in the bedroom

Chapter 5

The minute the front door closed, Julian took her in his arms and held her in a lover's embrace. He sniffed at her neck and her hair. "I love the way you smell, like fresh lilacs," he said softly. He scooped her up and carried her down the hall to the bedroom. Gliding over to the bed, he sat her down gently and placed kisses all over her body. He started undressing her; first taking off her shoes then worked his way up my legs to remove her hose. "You have the sexiest legs I've ever seen," he said. Truthfully, he had seen lots of women's legs in his time, though not in this manner. He had never undressed a female before. He was getting excited just knowing that his prize lay just between her legs. The next item he removed was her dress, which was form fitting. He had to help her shimmy out of it, which caused his pants to tighten in one particular spot. When he got to her bra and barely-there panties, the bulge in his pants grew even larger and was becoming painful.

Julian was about to lose control. He needed to hurry this up. He wanted inside her severely. The sight of her removing those last two items caused him to let out a strangled groan. Trinity chuckled, and said, "Are you alright big boy?" "Fine baby, I'm just fine," he answered. She chuckled again.

She watched as he took off his shirt. His chest was massive with a light smattering of dark hair straight down the middle, below his waistline. She couldn't help but notice that he was commando when he took off his pants. She gasped as her eyes widened at the width and length of his cock. She licked her lips and slid to the edge of the bed. She wanted to pleasure him with her mouth, but didn't think she could take all of him.

She stuck her tongue out and touched the tip of his cock. Julian stared down at her and moved closer. She licked up and down his enormous shaft gently sucking in places. The next thing he knew, his cock was enclosed in warmth. She took him into her mouth, circling the head with her tongue, drawing him deeper into her mouth. He clamped his jaw and stared down at her with hooded eyes as he pushed further in. He started to fuck her mouth in earnest. Her mouth was incredible and if he didn't stop this soon, he was going to lose it.

She cupped his sack, wrapped her hands around the base of his shaft and pumped as she sucked. She tasted the drops of fluid that came up to the head and dribbled out through the slit. His balls began to tighten. He knew that if he let this continue he was going to spill and he wasn't ready to do that yet. He clenched his jaw and pulled out of her mouth.

"Why did you stop me?" she asked. "You are amazing baby, but I want to be inside you when I come. I want to feel your legs wrapped around me, squeezing me when I let go. Move up the bed baby, I want to lie between your legs," he said. Julian could smell her arousal. As she moved, he could also see how large her jugular had become, knowing it was pulsing with her life force. He was tempted to lean in and nick her neck just for a little taste. Fighting temptation, he nibbled on her earlobe and lightly sucked her neck. Her moaning and twitching beneath him ramped up his arousal.

Julian couldn't take much more, he wanted inside of her now. Lifting her legs to his shoulders as he positioned himself to enter her sweet pussy, he put them back down and stared into her beautiful pools of blue, and with a gravelly voice said,

"Tell me what you want and how you want it baby."

"I want to give you what you want any way you want it," she said.

"I need to be with you baby, to love you. I need you to be with me," he insisted.

She touched her rosy nipples with her index fingers and said, "Here," as she put a finger in her mouth, licked it and touched her clit. "Here." Julian watched with dark hungry eyes as she inserted two fingers inside herself and finally said, "I want your cock here, inside me." He growled, lowered his head and began to caress and suck one nipple then the other. He felt the little pebbles grow and become hard on his tongue. Slowly sliding down her body, he looked up into her eyes, gave a lopsided smile then lowered his head. He licked her clit and flicked it around circling her nub. Trinity moaned and wiggled as she felt him latch on to her nub and suck hard. She bucked against his mouth, her nails digging into his broad shoulders. Trinity wrapped her legs around Julian's head. She was about to let go.

Julian felt her clit harden on his tongue. It was full of blood. He wanted to taste it so bad, but did not attempt to nick her for fear that he would not be able to stop at just a taste. He latched on to her clit and sucked hard. Inserting two fingers, she felt her arch up off the bed, shove her pussy hard into his mouth and screamed as she came. Her orgasm seemed to go on forever. He lapped up her cream and gently sucked until she was done.

Finally lowering her body back to the bed, she put her legs down, fisted a hand full of Julian's hair and just held on. She was trembling. She had never felt anything like that before. He raised his head just as she freed his hair, kissing her clean shaven mound, Julian slid back up her body, holding himself over her, stared into her eyes. His cock was so hard he thought it would burst. He positioned himself between her legs, closed his eyes then slammed into her, hard. She gasped and grabbed on to his arms, digging her nails into him and holding on tight as he rode her.

"Oh yes, please don't," she moaned.

"Don't what baby?" he asked.

"Don't stop. Please don't stop."

"Never, baby."

Julian fucked her so hard he was seeing stars. His balls were slapping into her ass and she was rocking back into him. She matched his strokes, arching up off the bed just as another orgasm rocked through her; she screamed his name, and felt him pump two more times then go still; he was filling her with his seed.

Julian rolled to his side, taking her with him and wrapping his arms around her. Their panting subsiding, she heard something in the hall. Julian moved with warp speed to the door and was about to open it to grab whoever was on the other side, when she heard a female voice gingerly call out to Trin. It was Sara. Though they couldn't see it, the smile that was in her voice was probably on her face when she asked if everything was alright.

"Yes, I'm ok, go back to sleep. I'll see you in the morning."

"Are you sure?" Sara asked with a giggle.

"Yes, I'm fine, go to bed." Trinity said.

The two of them laughed as Julian came back to bed. He held on to Trinity as though this was their last night together. She gazed over at Julian and smiled.

"Go ahead and ask, I know you have questions and I made a promise to you that I would answer them."

"Will you answer them honestly?" she asked.

"Yes. I don't lie, Trinity. I never have and I'm not about to start now.

"What do you want to know?"

"First, have you and your brother always been vampires? How old are you? What do you do for money? Where do you come from? Where do you live? Where is the rest of your family and are they vampires too? And finally, do you always stay hard because you are now?"

"Wow, woman, so many questions at one time."

"Okay, first, Marcel and I were born Hybrid Vampires." "My father is a vampire and my mother is human." "How does that work?" "My father met my mother when they lived in London. He was human when he first saw her and turned by a friend.

My father had no idea his friend was a vampire until the night of his changing. They had gone out for an evening of merriment and were accosted in one of London's many dark alleyways. My father was severely wounded. His friend always seemed to be alone except for my father, and since he didn't want to lose that friendship, he saved my father by turning him.

His friend explained what he had done and hoped my dad would understand. For a while, dad resented his strange new existence, but with the teachings of his friend, he learned to adjust. He quickly learned not to kill his victims, which they now call donors. Anyway, he formally met mother at a social gathering one evening and started visiting her with her father's permission. One night my mother discovered what he was. She was returning home from the theatre with her cousin and as they were about to climb the stairs to their house, she saw something off in the distance. Urging her cousin into the house, she went to investigate and stumbled upon two figures. She stepped closer and watched as one figure seemed to be biting the other. She then noticed the figures were two men and gasped as one of the men slumped over and was laid up against the wall. The other man was walking quickly toward her. He looked up and stared into her eyes. Mother backed away at first, but then sensing he would not hurt her, she asked if the man was dead. He told her no. It was then that my father told her the truth about himself. My mother never told anyone, she loved my father and he loved her. They were wed the traditional way a week later, and that same night he claimed her in vampire tradition as his blood mate. People began to suspect there was something different about my father and his friend, since they never left the house until sundown.

Their suspicions led my dad to believe it would be better if they left London. They all left together and journeyed to America. They settled in Rhode Island for a while, after some years, they moved here to New York." Julian explained, slowly.

"I suppose your father wanted to turn your mother."

"Yes, he did. They talked about it. He didn't turn her, though she would have let him. He decided to leave her human because they both wanted children. Female vampires can't have children, and I won't go into that right now because it's an even longer story than this one. Mother drinks his blood, which sustains her and he drinks from her only. If anything were to happen to my father, it would also be her end.

In answer to one of your other questions, I am the youngest. Marcel is Three Hundred Thirty-eight and I am Three Hundred Thirty-Five. It's just the two of us, though I suspect mother wanted a daughter but father decided to stop after two sons. Mother had a very hard time with me, and father didn't want to lose her.

My brother and I both own the Palace. I am the silent partner though; unless, I need to get involved. We share a home together. It's a rather large house. I live on one side of the house and my brother lives on the other side. We also let a few of our friends live there and before you ask, yes they are vampires and no, we don't sleep in coffins and have bats in the attic. I sleep in a bed, a very comfortable bed. I'll take you there one evening if you would like to see it. I won't answer your last question just yet, but I will."

"Julian, I have to ask you one more thing."

"Yes, I know."

"What do I have to do with your dreams?"   "

"Yes"

"Trinity, I was living in Rhode Island when you were. I watched over you then. Your dreams are not complete. You have parts missing, which will eventually come to you. That is when you will discover everything else."

"I don't have all of the details yet, but I promise you I will tell you everything if I discover it. In the meantime, I will always be near to protect you."

"Do you trust me to do that?" he asked intensely.

"Yes Julian, I do!" she replied.

"I have to leave now baby, but I will see you tonight. I'll be here, we have the weekend off. Should I use the window, since your friends don't know me yet, Julian said with a smirk?"

"Wipe that smirk off your face, and no, but they will tonight so use the door. Don't look at me like that. I'll just be making introductions, no background information. Is that to your liking?"

"Yes, okay, see you after 6:30pm."

Trin woke to a loud thump on the bedroom door and a lot of giggling on the other side of it.

"Trinity Elaine Parker, get up." "Come in ladies, I know what you're up to."

"So, where's mister marathon man?"

"What? What are you talking about Sara?"

"You know. I couldn't get back to sleep after that last one."

"Oh Sara, stop!!

"I heard the bed bounce off the wall. You know, Sara told me you were in there screaming and calling out some man's name. We all know it wasn't Colin so who was in there with you and where is he now?"

The three of them looked at each other as Trin said, "He left a while ago, and no, it was definitely not Colin." "Well who is this mystery man and where did you meet him?" Sara asked.

"I have never had a man make me feel the way Julian does."

With upturned lips, both Sara and Lisa replied in unison, "Oh Julian, huh?"

"We haven't known each other that long, but I've fallen for him, hard."

"Well, when do we get to meet him? Sara asked.

"Tonight, if you're lucky. He will be here around six-thirty or closer to seven."

The three burst into laughter.

"How do you feel about us inviting some friends over, we can make it a couples night?" Lisa asked.

"Sure, why not," Trinity replied.

"Ok, Sara I'm calling Andre first then you can call Arnaud," Lisa said.

"Just make one phone call Lisa, they live together," Trinity said.

"How do you know that?" Lisa asked.

"Andre told me last night that he and Arnaud share a place."

"Great!" Lisa said, as she jumped for the phone and missed.

"She's pouting Sara, give her the phone." Trinity said.

"Are you twenty-four or four?" Lisa said.

"Here, call your man," Sara insisted.

"When you two have finished, I need to call my brothers and check on them," Trinity said.

"Sure thing," Sara replied.

Lisa handed Trin the phone and left her alone in the room to speak with her brothers. Simon picked up on the first ring. "Hi sis, what's up?" "I just wanted to see how things were going with Scott being there." "He's fine, been hanging out with Colin." "What? Why? Have you been that busy?" "No. Colin came by to talk, said you two had a big argument, and were taking a time out so he's been coming by here and showing some brother-in-law love to Scott." "Don't call him that. We are not getting married. In fact, we are not getting back together. I don't trust him Simon. Something's wrong. I just can't put my finger on it." "I'll watch him with Scott from now on. I trust your judgment sis.

By the way, Jason Foster is back in town. He has a wife. I think you know her, Courtney." "Wow, miss popular herself. When did that happen?" "They apparently caught up with each other in California, dated a few times then tied the knot. He said they are looking for a house here. He is a lawyer now and has joined Mr. Butler's firm." "Well, that explains a lot. Simon, I've got to go, I just wanted to check in."

"Look sis, stay there for a while. Scott is fine here with me and Alex. Besides, I don't want you two out at the house all week alone." "What's going on Simon?" "I don't know. Just some strange goings on in the area that's all." "Like what?" "I saw a couple of people walking around like zombies. I knew who they were, but they were in some kind of haze. It took this one guy a while before he could remember who he was, then it all clicked and he was fine again. I don't like it and would feel better if you just stayed put. Now that that's settled, enjoy yourself and I'll have Scott call you when he finally gets up for the day."

"Okay, tell Alex hello; I will, bye."

Trinity hung up the phone and darted out of her room, singing as she went toward the living room. "Well ladies it looks like I'll be staying with my bff's for a while longer if you two have no objections." "Are you kidding?" They were ecstatic about the news and toasted with a glass of orange juice as they prepared for a night that promised to be fun and more. She also filled them in on the rest of her conversation with Simon and the fact that Jason was in town with his wife. They were not shocked that he married Courtney. "Ok ladies, enough about those two, let's get ready for some fun."

The apartment was busy with the three of them getting ready for their dates; they tried hogging the mirror to put on makeup and fix their hair, while carrying on a three-way conversation.

Sara was first to enter the living room, she slipped on a long sleeved light blue blouse with frills around the collar and cuffs, and navy blue ankle length skirt with a slit up the back that revealed long slender legs, and a pair of four-inch pumps. Lisa was in an ankle length pale green scoop neck dress with a slit up the front; her shoes were beige four-inch pumps with a peek-a-boo toe. Finally, Trinity came out in a floor length tapered red dress with spaghetti straps that dipped in the front to reveal the outline of her full breasts; the slit up the side showed off her long silky sexy legs and the black sling back heels she wore made her look as though she were at least six feet tall. All three women wore their hair up in a bun. They were all beautiful in their own way. Trinity's raven hair and blue eyes gave her the look of elegance; Lisa's blonde hair and sexy pale blue eyes gave her the look of the lady of the manor, and Sara with her fiery red hair and green eyes gave her the look of someone who could be a heartbreaker.

The doorbell rang, and when Lisa answered it, she saw all three tall, broad, strikingly handsome men standing there. After being invited in, they entered and went to their respective partners. Andre and Arnaud whistled at the sight of the women; Julian gave Trinity a look that made her want to jump in his arms and wrap her legs around him and fuck him right there.

Knowing what was on her mind, he gave her a lopsided smile, held her in his arms and laid one of his panty melting kisses on her. Andre and Arnaud were as big and broad as Julian. Trin wondered if they might be vampires as well, then she put the thought out of her mind.

The five of them greeted each other as friends since they worked together. The guys shared living quarters in Julian and Marcel's home, but no one else knew that. Trin introduced Julian to her friends. Once the greetings were done, they headed out the door. The six of them took in a show and went to one of the swanky clubs in mid-town Manhattan. Julian was recognized the minute he walked through the door and they were quickly seated in one of the larger booths. This was one of his special places to patronize, drink, and search for donors. Drink orders were taken, and while they were waiting for their drinks, they all laughed at Andre's corny jokes.

Lisa wanted to dance and asked her friends to join her on the floor. "You all go and have fun, I'll be here when you finish. Don't you dance Julian?" asked Lisa. "Yes, but not to that music. I'm more of a slow groove type." "Oh, ok. Well we can take turns dancing with Trinity, if you don't mind." Arnaud heard a low growl come from Julian. He stepped away and said, "Maybe you should stay here with your date. She smiled because she heard the growl as well. "I think you're right Arnaud, we'll watch you guys dance." They all agreed and Trin watched as her friends stepped out on the dance floor with all the other gyrating bodies, which seemed to be oblivious to the loud music.

The drinks arrived while the others were on the dance floor; and as she was about to raise her glass and take a drink, she spotted Colin coming through the door. "Oh no, I can't take this crap tonight." What? Him, and she pointed toward the door. Julian turned to see Colin coming toward them.

The drinks arrived while the others were on the dance floor; and as she was about to raise her glass and take a drink, she spotted Colin coming through the door.

"Oh no, I can't take this crap tonight."

"What?"

"Him," and she pointed toward the door. Julian turned to see Colin coming toward them. Sara and Lisa saw him and stopped dancing; they rushed from the dance floor with Andre and Arnaud following close behind. The guys stood at Julian's left and right flank while the girls stood near their friend. Colin stepped to Trin, who was standing by the time he reached the group.

"We need to talk," Colin stated as he pressed Trinity into the wall adjacent to the booth they had been sitting in.

"Leave her alone," Andre yelled in a frosty tone.

"Tell your friends to back off."

"Get off of me dickhead." Trinity said.

Colin leaned down with a smirk on his face and tried to kiss her. Trinity gritted her teeth as she felt herself being yanked forward. Lisa caught her just before she fell. She looked up and saw Colin in Julian's grip. "I'm only going to tell you this once. **LEAVE HER ALONE!**"

"Fuck off dude." Colin said.

"Colin, do you really want to do this here?"

"She's my girlfriend."

"She may have been at one time, but she's with me now so I suggest you leave before this gets really ugly," Julian said as he loosed his grip on Colin and backed away.

"I'll catch up with you later, Trin and as for you three, you better watch your backs."

After making that snarky statement, he left. The club was quiet with all eyes on them, especially Julian and Colin. Everyone was waiting to see what was going to happen next. Once the excitement was over, the music started to play and the dance floor began to fill up again with twirling bodies.

The group decided to leave and head to the Palace. Julian wanted to see his brother and warn him about the night's events. The restaurant was just as busy as the club they had left. People were enjoying food, drink, and conversation. Trin and her friends took a booth upstairs, while Julian and Marcel went in the back to the soundproof office. The two made plans to meet up later after Trinity and her friends were safely back home. They needed to find out just what Colin was up to.

Two nights later, the trip to Rhode Island would reveal all. Giles called a meeting with Bill and Charlie. Giles didn't know he had been followed. The meeting took place as before, in the obscurities of a warehouse. "The Parker girl has hired an attorney."
"Who?" Charlie asked.
"Is he any good."

"I know his reputation. Giles said. Tristan Winslow is no slouch. He's one of those do-gooder types, and will look out for her interests. However, I also know his partner well. Andrea Campbell. She is my operative. She was bought in on the girl's case and will keep me informed. I just have to get my son to straighten his head out where she is concerned and somehow get her here when the time comes."

"She still doesn't know that Colin is your son?"

"No and I hope to keep it that way until the last minute."

Bill began, "Look, I say we move now Giles. She could sell and we wouldn't know it until after the sale is done."

"What are you worried about, Bill? You're still making money off the sale of the stuff you move aren't you?" Giles asked."

"Yeah, but somebody's gonna get wise to the higher than usual prices we charge. We have to be careful and know the laws for some of the places we do business."

"That's where I come in." Giles said, I've taken care of you up until now haven't I Charlie? Bill?"

"Yes, but we still need to be careful," Charlie said.

"I have this covered; you keep doing what you're doing. I should have a progress report this afternoon. She's seeing Winslow today. After that, depending on how far they've gotten with selling, will determine when the rest will happen."

****

Julian looked at his surroundings and realized he was standing in the place he saw in Trinity's dreams. He realised that she was in real danger and why. She owned the business her father left her, the pharmaceutical company and these men, friends of her father's, were going to kill her for the company in order to keep making profits from illegally manufactured drugs. One of her lawyer's is in on the deal as well as her family's lawyer and friend. Julian knew that he would have to keep a close eye on Trinity now as well as her brothers. Once he returned home he would inform his brother and their friends of his news.

Julian needed to make his way out of the warehouse before he was discovered. Having heard enough to know that these men would meet one more time before they planned to make their move unless there was a turn of events, he would head back home and wait. He would not be able to find out anything further until he rose for the evening, but he would be sure to ask Trinity without arousing too suspicion. He arrived back home before first light and summoned his brother and friends to meet in their living room. Julian told them what he had found out by following Giles to Rhode Island.

"That's where all this began?"

"Yes brother and it will end there. I learned one other little tidbit." "That is what, don't keep us in suspense?" "Colin is Giles' son." "What?" "Exactly! And Andrea Campbell is in with them."

"We have to stop them Jules." Marcel said.

"I know Mar. We're going to need a few more friends to help with this one." "Can we count on Jade and Rowena?"

"Yes, I'll let them know and fill them in on everything," Andre said.

"We need to watch everything that Colin and his father do, "Julian said.

Andre looked at him and asked, "What about Andrea Campbell?"

Marcel replied, "Let the ladies handle her and we will take care of the others. One more detail---the bodyguard."

"Not a problem guys, big brawn over there will have that one covered."

"Big Brawn?" Nicky said.

Just then Jade's mate walked into the room. He was as tall as the other four and all muscle. Julian smiled and said, good to see you Nicky. It's about time you showed up."

"Yeah I know, but that last job you assigned me to was a bit sticky, I'm just glad all's well that ends well with that one, you know."

"Are we on to something else already or is this the same thing you've been working on for a while?" In unison, everyone answered, "It's the same thing." There was a brief sound of laughter in the room from everyone except Julian. Nicky resumed speaking; I'm assuming she knows who you are for all of this protection. Have either of you claimed her yet?" The roar that came from Julian was so forceful that Nicky backed up from where he stood.

"Well, I guess that means she belongs to you then huh Jules?"

"Get stuffed Nick"!!

Marcel laid the situation out for Nicky. "We'll go into action at sunset." "Fine, but I need to see my mate first. I need to get laid and I'm sure she does too by now. Where is she by the way, I didn't see her when I came in through the tunnel?" "Jade stayed at the Palace. She's locked in the spare room behind the office. She's fine in there." "I'll let her rest then. We have plenty of time to be together. Besides, I need to clean up before I see her."

The office phone rang for what seemed like forever. Jade was in no mood to talk to anyone. She wanted to be home and safe in the arms of her mate. She missed Nicky so much. While she was lost in thought, the phone rang again. She answered, hi baby, the voice on the other end said.

"Oh, Nicky!"

"Come home soon baby, I've missed you. I need you."

"I will Nicky, as soon as the sun sets, I will."

Chapter 6

The dream began as all others had, with Trinity calling out for help and running through a warehouse. There was that chemical smell again. It was the same odor as in her other dreams. She ran as she had before, hearing footsteps then voices. Someone was calling out Colin's name. She peeked out from where she was hidden and noticed Colin standing in the middle of the floor with a knife in his hand and a killer look on his face.

I need to get out of here, and she stepped out into the open to run. Before she could take off, she spotted Julian. She saw movement to her left and looked around just in time to see Colin coming toward Julian with the knife raised in his right hand. She heard other footsteps in the warehouse. Colin was running straight for Julian. He stabs at Julian. Just then she screamed and woke up, sitting straight up in the bed as Sara and Lisa ran into her room.

"Another bad dream Trin?" Sara asked.

"Yes and it's worse than the last one."

"Is the medication helping you any?"

"I thought it was, but now I'm not so sure anymore."

"When do you see doctor Marshall again?" Lisa asked.

"I have an appointment for this afternoon at 2:00pm. Good, we'll go with you.

The next day, Trinity called her job to remind Aria that she would be coming to work a little later. Trinity Sara and Lisa reached Doctor Marshall's office fifteen minutes early, the receptionist told her to have a seat and the doctor would be with her shortly. "Thanks Debbie, Trinity said.

After a few minutes, the attending aid came out and call Trinity's name. She was seated and her vitals were taken just as her doctor walked in. "Hello Trinity," "Hi Doc Jane." "How are you feeling, you look tired." "I had another dream and this one was worse than the last." "Are you using the techniques and taking your medication?", Dr. Marshall asked.

"Yes, but it doesn't seem to be working". Do you want to talk to me about what was in your dream? No because whatever that is, I don't want it to come true. Well, Trinity, whatever it was, I don't think there's much chance of that happening. I'm going to increase the dosage of your medication and have you come back in two weeks. Let's see what happens with the increased dosage.

You also need to take a few days off and get some rest. I have this weekend off, maybe I can get some undisturbed sleep. I hope that when you return in two weeks, the meds have worked and you have rested. She stopped at the receptionist's desk to make yet another appointment and headed to the drugstore with my best friends to get my prescription filled. Sara, can you stay and get my medication? I need to see my attorney and Lisa is going to go with me. Sure, you two go ahead, I'll meet you back home.

****

The guard in the lobby of the Winslow building notified Mr. Winslow that Trinity was on her way up to his office. She and Lisa ran into Andrea Campbell in the hallway. They walked into Tristan Winslow's office together. Hello ladies, please have a seat. Can I offer you something to drink? No thank you Mr. Winslow, they said.

I know that we had an appointment for later today, but I thought it would be better for me, since I was already in the neighborhood, to stop by now, I hope that's okay with you. Yes, that's fine. I have some free time. What can I do for you? Do you have good news for me yet? Yes, as a matter of fact, I do. I have been contacted by several prospective buyers who are interested in acquiring the company your father left you. If you want, I can set up meetings with the parties and take their bids. That won't be necessary, sell it today, and it doesn't matter who you sell it to. The money doesn't matter to me either. I don't need that company; and everyone that worked for my father was compensated very well.

Ms. Campbell, Ms. James, would you please excuse us, I need to speak with Ms. Parker alone, Tristan said. Just wait in the outer office or in your office Ms. Campbell, thanks!! With raised eyebrows, Andrea and Lisa stepped out of the office, closing the door tightly behind them.

Trinity, let me say that I am first and foremost your attorney and hopefully a friend. I have been taken into confidence and will not break the trust of the one who confided in me.

Tristan, what is this about? Trinity, what I'm about to tell you must stay within these walls. I received a note this afternoon from someone I know well. I believe you two are acquainted as well. She sat there with a puzzled look on her face waiting for the punch line. I'll show you the note but I need your word that you will not discuss this with anyone. Can you make me that promise, Trinity? "Yes, Yes, I promise!!

Here, read the note, I have covered the name of the person who wrote the note: *Without going into a lot of detail Tristan, I must warn you that Andrea Campbell is a plant. She has been monitoring your dealings with Trinity Parker. Please guard Ms. Parker and her interests with your life for she is in danger from those who claim to be close to her family. I will do my best to explain to explain in more detail when I see you. Keep Trinity out of harm's way.*

As always,

Your friend

The shocked look on her face said it all. I take it you know my friend. Yes, we know each other. Then you should know what's at stake should you reveal any knowledge of this note. Yes! I'll be seeing Julian tonight. He can explain the rest. In the meantime, I'll take you and your friend home, it's on my way. I need to make sure you get home safely. Let me make a few phone calls while you're here and see if we can't unload the company now.

****

She didn't dare make a call from her desk phone. Andrea excused herself, feigning a mild headache and the need to get some aspirin; she rushed to her office to call Giles Butler. She hit the auto dial on her cell phone, one ring and he picked up.

Recognizing the number in his caller ID, Giles immediately said "Hello Andrea, there'd better be a damn good reason for this call."

"You sound so cheerful, who did you stomp on today?"

"I don't need any of your snarky remarks, what do you want now?" "It can't be money, I thought I paid you enough money to last a lifetime." Giles remarked.

"I don't want anything else from you, I'm reporting in. We had a visitor today, as a matter of fact we still do."

"She's there now?

"Ah, now you want to talk."

"Winslow is about to sell that company she owns.

"Why aren't you in there with them?"

"Winslow asked me to leave so he could talk to her alone, you Ass."

"There's no need for you to keep up the smart remarks Andrea. Just realise things for what they were and move on."

"What Giles? You used me then and you're using me now."

"You let me, Andrea, and you have been paid handsomely for all services rendered.   You were a great lay then, but you started spreading it around. I had no need for you after that. The whore in you enjoyed it too. I don't want to stroll down memory lane with you today so let's get on with what this call is about. You should get yourself back into that office, find out if the sale has been made, and get back in touch."

Andrea hung up and went back to the outer office, Lisa was still sitting there. She knocked on Winslow's door and cracked it asking if he had concluded his meeting. Tristan was just hanging up the phone; he motioned for her to come in, she signaled Lisa to rejoin them.

We have sold Ms. Parker's company for a considerable amount of money. The sale is final and the owners will be taking possession right away. I need you to prepare the necessary contracts and bring them in to me Andrea. But Mr. Winslow, this is highly irregular. Just bring me the contracts, now Andrea. She rushed to her office, shaking. The tone of his voice was unnerving. Tristan had never spoken to her in that abrupt tone before today. She wondered if he knew she was a plant. He couldn't have gained that information from anyone, the only person who held that information was waiting for her return call. Andrea returned with the required contracts and quickly left Winslow's office.

Once the documents were signed a duplicate copy was given to Trin. Tristan rose and said now that our business has concluded let me see you ladies home. As they headed toward the elevators, Lisa noticed Andrea watching them step into the elevator while she was speaking on the phone. She wondered what that look was about.

****

The air was crisp and clear. It was late March. Jade knew when the sun faded in the sky. She made her way home to Nicky. He was waiting for her at the top of the stairs when she bounced in the house. She started up the staircase stopping midway to look up, their eyes met. She stared into his beautiful golden gaze and he gave a seductive stare into her almond shaped jade green ones. He rushed down the steps and scooped her up in his arms.

"Jade." Nicky said as he walked down the stairs to his mate.

Nicky took the steps two at a time getting back up the stairs and to their room. Once they closed the door behind them, Nicky made quick work of getting out of his clothes. We'll talk later he said, first things first. He looked over at Jade sitting on the bed undressing. She had taken off her pants and top and was about to lay against the pillows when Nicky walked over and said, "You have too many clothes on love," I want you completely naked. Take your bra and panties off now; unless you want me to take them off----should that be the case they will be destroyed because I'll rip them from your body. She held her breath, the thought of him ripping anything off of her made her wetter than she already was. Her desire was rapidly growing. She wanted to feel him inside of her. She needed him.

They didn't have rough sex the way they usually did. He wanted to tenderly love his mate. Let her know that they didn't always have to be rough with each other. They held each other in a tight embrace, their fangs extended, Nicky licked her neck then bit down; the taste of her blood flowing into him, reinforcing him. Jade placed her lips on his shoulder and punctured him just below the shoulder blade. His life sustaining fluid flowed into her as they gently rocked each other into release. Afterward, they licked the bite marks on each other to seal the skin. They lay still, holding each other. Not moving, not speaking; just holding and feeling.

****

The minute she walked into the apartment, she felt his presence. Her head was still dizzy from reading that note in Tristan's office. She headed toward the bedroom when Lisa stopped her. What's wrong? You haven't been yourself since we left Mr. Winslow's office. What did he say to you? Lisa, I can't talk about it right now. I will explain everything to you and Sara later, but now, I need to contact Julian.

Julian was standing in her bedroom waiting. He knew he needed to tell her what was about to happen. He had to get through to her the fact that her life was in danger without her thinking he was crazy. When Trinity opened the door, she took two steps and felt a hand on her arm. He pulled her through the door, spun her around in his arms and planted a fierce kiss on her lips. Once the fog cleared from her brain, she pushed him away. You can't silence my questions by kissing me like that Julian. I know! You need to start explaining what that cryptic note meant now because whatever this is will mean nothing if I find that I can't trust you either because I sure as hell don't trust Colin. It's good that you don't trust him or anyone related to him. "Explain." I will while we're driving to my house. I need to get you out of here. I have a question for you, Trinity. What note are you talking about?

Tristan Winslow, my lawyer handed me a note to read, he covered the name but the paper was thin. I still saw the name, it was you. I need you to please tell me what's going on. I intend to Trinity, lets get out of here.

Julian drove for the better part of an hour. The house was just on the edge of the city. He parked the car in the garage adjoining what looked like an old Victorian Manson. By the time they arrived at his house, he had explained the reason for the note and Andrea's part the scheme of things. When they stepped through the front door, she noticed how beautiful it was. The walls were paneled in rich dark wood, the floor to ceiling windows were covered with dark blackout curtains and the floors also looked of a rich dark wood. The staircase was done in red with soft lighting throughout. She also noticed that everyone was sitting in the study. She knew all of the faces in the room except one. Who was he? She thought he must be related to the brothers in some way since he was just as big though he had bronze skin and golden eyes instead of chocolate brown.

"Trinity, this is Nick Russell, our cousin," Julian said.

"Just call me Nicky." So, you're the one who has stolen our Jules's heart, and from the way you keep looking up at him. I think those feelings are mutual, yes? She turned beet red from Nicky's comment. Ahh look at that, she blushes too. Don't be embarrassed, you're among friends here. So human, Nicky thought!!

Julian urged everyone to take a seat. We have things to discuss. "Jules, what have you told Trinity so far?" Marcel asked. "Only the part Andrea Campbell is playing in this, Julian answered. "Trinity still doesn't understand why Colin and I have been so prevalent in her dreams," Julian continued.

"Help her out then Jules explain it to her now."

"Fine Nick!"

Julian began telling Trinity that he had been tracking Colin's movements for some time now and just recently, started looking at her shady family lawyer. "Giles Butler", she asked. Yes!

"Jules followed Giles to Rhode Island a few nights ago and stumbled onto his big plans for you, Marcel stated. First, you need to know that Giles and Colin are related. They are father and son.

"Giles never spoke of children," Trinity added. He always went out of the country twice a year with his wife. She assumed they were on vacation, but they must have been visiting Colin away at school.

Trinity was beyond shocked by the time she heard everything Julian, Marcel and Nicky had to say. "So let me get this straight, they want to kill me because I was selling my father's company." "But why?"

"The men you knew as your dad's friends and partners, along with Giles were pushing illegal pharmaceuticals through the textile company and making a big profit, and the sale of the company would halt all of that," Julian added.

Trinity couldn't believe what she was hearing. She told them that the company had been sold earlier in the day and the new owners were flying there to inspect it.

"That's the information Andrea Campbell was waiting for" Julian belted out. She has probably already informed Giles. "As of tonight, you are not to be alone Trinity." Julian spoke up; you will have to stay here with us until this is over."

Just as Trinity started to protest, her phone rang. She saw Simon's name in the caller ID and answered. Before she could say anything, he yelled in the phone, Scott's gone sis, Colin took him. She became hysterical; took him where Simon? I found a note when Alex and I got home.

"What are you talking about Simon, what note?" Trinity asked.

"What does the note say Simon?"

"You know who we are, you know what we want; you are the key."

"GIVE THEM WHAT THEY WANT SIS," Simon yelled in the phone.

"The note said that you know what they want sis." "Who are they and what is it that they want?" Simon asked. Trinity dropped the phone and screamed "Colin has taken my little brother."

Marcel picked up the phone and put it on speaker as he spoke to Simon so everyone could hear. Simon read the contents of the note. Marcel told Simon that Trinity would be safe where she is and their brother would be found, he also urged Simon to take his girlfriend some place safe.

"I can't let you do this, Trinity said. I have to rescue my brother and if that means letting them take me that's the way it will have to be."

"Julian's roar startled her. "NO." YOU. ARE. MINE. And you always will be. I'll protect you and we'll get Scott back," he said.

Nicky told her that the seven of them would be working together to get him back. So you're all vampires then? Trinity asked.

"Yes, but you knew that when you walked into this room." Nicky answered. She acknowledged that other than Julian, Marcel and Nicky, the other four were a surprise.

"Julian, what am I going to tell my friends, they're going to know something is up?" Trinity asked. We tell each other just about everything. "Andre and Arnaud can take care of that for you," Julian said.

"We need to make a plan of action," Jade and Rowena said in unison. We don't have the luxury of time, so somebody start talking, get your ideas out on the table. Trinity looked around the room then said; don't even think about excluding me from this, Scott's my brother.

"Not on your life baby." I can't let you get captured, they intend to kill you and maybe both your brothers as well. Julian, I have to. I just have to. They looked into each other's eyes long and hard and he understood. Julian looked at his brother then back at Trinity and nodded his ok.

The plan came together perfectly, though Julian didn't like the part Trinity had to play, the prey. They didn't know who would be coming after her though they suspected it would be Colin, so everyone had to be ready to move at a moment's notice. After the meeting concluded, everyone went about their way.

"Can I get you anything baby?"

"No, Julian," but you can show me around your house. If the rest of it looks anything like the study, I know it's beautiful. The only room I want to show you right now is my bedroom. What'd you have in mind?

"Let us go upstairs and I'll show you," Julian answered.

Julian showed Trinity the way to his room. When he opened the door and turned on the lights, she saw a huge bed sitting in the middle of the floor with a canopy and black curtains that circled it. The floor was dark mahogany wood to match the dark paneled walls and blackout curtains at each of the floor to ceiling windows. He led the way to the bathroom, and when she stepped in, she felt as though she had walked into another time. The circular shower could easily fit a football team with its pale blue walls. The pale blue bathtub had a Jacuzzi with old world designs around it. The room was large enough to put her apartment inside it and still be able to walk around without bumping into anything. Strangely, there was something missing, mirrors. There were none to be found in his room either and she suspected there were none in the entire house. Trinity felt comfortable being there.

"Now that we are alone, I need to ask you something, Julian."

"Anything, my lady!"

"Am I your lady?"

"Do you want me as much as I want you, Julian?"

"What kind of question is that? Of course I want you, more than I've ever wanted anything in my entire being."

"Trinity, I have only ever been with two others and they were the same as I am. You are the first human and the only woman I have ever fallen in love with. Mother used to worry about me not being interested in any of the females my brother invited to be in our company. She finally gave up and said that things would happen in their own time. She was right. I've waited for what seems like an eternity and at last, it has happened. YOU!! I love you Trinity, more than life itself."

From what I've read about vampires, you haven't claimed me as your mate. I want you to bite me, Julian.

"Are you asking to become a vampire Trinity?"

"Yes, Julian." I want to be with you forever.

"I want that too, Trinity.

"I couldn't take losing you if I tried to turn you and something went horribly wrong. I wouldn't want to live without you, now that I have found you, my one and only true love."

"I feel as though I can never get enough of you, and when we're apart, I constantly think of you, and I find myself smiling.

"Come lay on the bed with me Trinity. Take your clothes off if you wish."

Trinity took everything off as did Julian. They stood before each other, naked, wanting. They climbed onto the bed and sat in the middle facing one another, her legs in between his; he reached out to pull her closer and kissed her ever so gently.

"I want you baby." I want to hear you say "please take me."

"I want you to tell me where and how you want me."

"I want your wetness on my face, your juices on my tongue and your lilac scent covering me."

"I want to feel your legs wrapped around me as we come together, and when I'm done with you, I will have left my scent on you, marking you as mine, because you are mine; you belong to me and you always will, Trinity."

Julian eased Trinity back on the bed, his muscular arms holding him up, his long untamed strands of inky black hair falling in front of him, teasing her forehead; he licked her neck, pressing his body against hers. Trinity closed her eyes holding him tight, wanting him to kiss her. Julian knew what she wanted but held back.

"Open your eyes baby, I want to gaze into your beautiful blue eyes and you into mine as I take you."

Julian kissed Trinity with such fervor that she thought she would come then and there. She felt him moving, teasing her slit until she opened her legs waiting for him to enter. He reared up and positioned himself between her legs, still staring into her eyes.

"Look at me baby," Julian said.

The minute she did, he slammed into her core. Raising up off the bed and clamping down on his shoulders, she couldn't hold on, she felt it coming. Trinity screamed as her orgasm rocked through her; it was a toe curling orgasm. Julian grabbed a hand full of Trinity's hair and pulled calling out her name as he came.

"Damn woman, you're going to be the death of me and I'm already dead, he chuckled.

Trinity gave Julian a smack on the arm, that's not even funny Julian, she stated. He laughed even harder then. "Lay with me baby, we only have a few more hours together before we have to go to work."

Chapter 7

When Bill Hogate and Charlie Anson stepped off the private plane, a car was waiting to take them straight to the warehouse district where Giles had been patiently waiting with his prisoner, Scott Parker. He couldn't get his hands on Trinity at the time, so his next move was to grab a member of her family. Luckily, Colin was able to handle that task and leave a note with explicit instructions for her to follow. He also had to get his accomplices to New York, so he sent his private jet for them. Colin and Chadwick were to get the girl later that night after she got off from work. That would be the easiest way. This has to end tonight, Giles said to himself. Just then, Bill and Charlie walked through the door.

"What's going on that we had to come here? Bill asked.

"The company was sold out from under us today and the new owners are there now, inspecting the place," Giles replied. "I hope you two cleaned up your mess."

"We did, but we need that company back," Bill answered again. "We have a lot of people to take care of, and some of them have paid us in advance."

"I have a little present waiting in the office over there," Giles mentioned.

"What now Giles?" Carlie asked.

"I have a member of the Parker family, the younger brother. Colin snatched him this afternoon from the other brother's place and left instructions for her to follow. So, we will be seeing her tonight if they ever want to see this one again."

"Where is the plant?" Charlie asked.

"Not to worry, I've already taken care of that little matter as well, Giles stated.

****

Arnaud and Andre arrived at Sara's front door in time to take her and Lisa to work.

"Where's Trin, Lisa asked? Andre spoke up, she's coming with Julian. The girls felt that something was wrong, but they wouldn't voice it, at least not yet and not to them. Their shift was in full swing and there was still no Trin. Marcel and Aria came in an hour later. Lisa asked him if he had seen their friend. His only reply was that she would be late. Lisa grabbed Sara into the back room and whispered in her ear, we've got to get to the bottom of things; we're not going to get any answers here. Something's happening with Trin and we need to find out what it is.

Rowena was passing the room the girls were talking in and overheard their conversation. She stepped in as they were about to walk out. Ladies, I overheard you talking. There are things that you don't know and wouldn't understand even if you did know. And as much as you want to help your friend, you will only end up hurting the situation so please stay out of it. Trinity will come to you for your help if she needs it. "But do not and I repeat, do not interfere." Rowena said. Huh, Lisa bellowed and stomped out into the hall while Sara turned to Rowena, looking her square in the eyes and said, "If anything happens to our friend, we will hold you and anyone connected with whatever has happened responsible." Rowena nodded and then stepped away, walking down the hall without turning around.

What do we do now Sara? We wait Lisa, we wait. They went back out to the floor to work their shift. As they walked out onto the floor, Lisa spotted Trinity coming from upstairs. She and Sara ran up to her and pulled her to the side. What's going on Trin? they asked. "I can't tell you now, Trinity said. I will explain everything to you when I can, but in the meantime, I will be staying with Julian and Marcel. I will be fine so please don't ask me anymore questions."

"Please." Trinity said again.

"If you need our help with anything Trin, just say the word because we will be with you all the way." Lisa said.

The restaurant was just closing when Colin walked through the door. He took quick inventory of the patrons, while searching out Trinity. When he saw her coming from the back, he said nothing, just stared at her for a long minute, then turned and walked back out the door. She knew from the look on his face that whatever was to happen to her would take place this night.

Julian sat hidden on the upper level of the restaurant. He saw Colin come in and survey the place and leave once he saw what or who he was looking for. Arnaud and Rowena alerted the others. They were ready for what was to happen this night. Trin went about her normal routine. She was trying to hold it together; she was nothing but a bundle of nerves, but when the time came, she would do her part. Her life and the life of her brother depended on it.

****

Colin and Chadwick, Giles's son and bodyguard, were waiting in the alley across the street, hidden in the shadows, waiting for her to come out. Her friends and staff always left ahead of her. "Do you have the cloth and chloroform ready Chadwick," because we will have to be quick?

"Yeah man, I know what to do." Chadwick said.

"Wait till she steps away from the door then grab her. Don't give her too much of that stuff; just enough to knock her out. I want her conscience when I take my revenge out on her. I want her to know who did it and why," Colin mumbled.

Trinity saw them approach on her left as she turned to walk away. Colin stopped her while the stranger he was with grabbed her from behind. He put a cloth over her nose, she could smell something strange in the cloth covering her nose, and then she went out like a light. She regained consciousness, and looked around only to discover she was in the trunk of a car, which added to her fear. She gulped the lump that had formed in her throat. Her heart began to sink as she thought, oh no, oh no, girl, you're trapped. She could feel it moving fast, hitting bumps and making sharp turns. Her hands and legs were tied, which kept her from kicking the lid of the trunk, her mouth was also covered with masking tape. Trinity thought that if she could make some kind of sound, it would alert anyone who may be out and about.

Suddenly, the car came to an abrupt stop, she heard two car doors slam closed, then she heard footsteps; they were coming to open the trunk. Once the trunk was opened, Colin untied her legs and lifted her out and stood her up.

"Lets take a walk," and he motioned to the door on their immediate right.

Trinity noticed that they were in the warehouse district. Then it hit her, this was the place in her dreams. Colin turned briefly to call out to Chadwick, move the car then join us inside. So, that was his name, Chadwick. She made a mental note for later. Colin turned back and pushed her through the door. Move, there are people here who want to see you, and we have some unfinished business to take care of. If she could have spoken at that moment, she would have told him in no uncertain terms to "GO TO HELL."

****

Marcel and Andre were parked a block down the street from the restaurant. They left by the back door, knowing who was in the alley across the street. They were undetected as they made their way to the car to sit and wait for the signal. Once the saw Colin they knew what the next move was going to be. Andre sent text messages to the others telling everyone to be ready, Trinity had just been taken. They would follow at a safe distance. Everyone's cars were equipped with GPS and able to track the miniscule device that was placed on Trinity's body earlier in the evening. They would know how and where to find her. They were ready. Julian led the precession; he needed to get to his mate before it was too late. Marcel followed close behind, hoping against all hope that Trinity was not harmed, for if she was, there would be hell to pay once his brother's wrath was let loose. They were driving 100mph heading toward the warehouse district, and their possible destruction.

****

Trinity noticed row after row of barrels and she noticed that all too familiar odor as they walked through the warehouse, finally coming to a stop near an office door. She saw her brother Scott, tied to a chair just inside the office. Giles Butler stepped out with two other men. She recognized them right away, friends and partners of her father. Nicky, Julian and Marcel had been right about them.

Colin walked toward Giles, greeting him with Trinity in tow.

"Dad," he greeted.

"Son," Giles greeted back.

"Take the tape off her mouth son, so she can speak. We have things to discuss then you can do with her as you wish."

Trinity stared at the two of them and noticed how much alike they looked. She knew then without a doubt that they were father and son. Colin removed the tape by snatching it hard and fast. She thought he was trying to take her lips off along with the skin on her face. Tears welled up in her eyes and he stood there with a self-satisfying smirk at the sight of her pain.

"This is just the beginning, it's going get a lot worse" Colin said, and then turned his head to laughed as Scott yelled "leave my sister alone you pig."

"Chadwick, take the brother and put him over by the barrels; keep him tied up. Put her in the office and leave me alone with her. We have a few things to talk over" Giles said. Trinity sat anxiously biting her lower lip waiting for Giles to speak.

"Trinity, we can do this the easy way, or you can make it hard for yourself; either way, this will end here tonight.

"Giles, what could I possibly have that you want?" she asked.

She felt as though her face exploded. He slapped her so hard, it almost turned her head.

"Lets not play games. I know you sold the company, and what I want to know is to who?"

"I need the papers that you signed Trinity."

While Giles handled things in the office, Chadwick stood guard at the front of the warehouse, Bill and Charlie stood as lookouts at the back. Colin ducked in between the barrels, keeping Scott in view. He had hidden a knife behind the barrels and kept it in sight and ready for use. Colin wondered what was taking his father so long. He wanted revenge for what Trinity had put him through and he wanted that revenge now.

Marcel and Julian reached the warehouse district at the same time, the others were close behind. They parked on the street so their car engines would not be heard. Once everyone was there, they gathered for a quick briefing from Nicky; then went into action taking their cue from Julian. Everyone spread out with Marcel and Nicky each taking a door, Jade and Arnaud were to go through the open window on far the side of the warehouse, leaving Rowena to come in through the roof. Julian staged a fight with Andre, just on the other side of the warehouse, which was the signal for everyone to move in.

Colin heard the commotion outside and alerted his father. All of a sudden, the doors blew off, glass shattered, guns were being fired and bodies were flying through the air. Chadwick picked himself up off the floor, fired his gun in Marcel's direction and missed, which only pissed the vampire off. With warp speed, he rushed the bodyguard, grabbing him and latching on to his neck, draining him dry. He then turned to find his brother, but spotted Scott instead, still tied up sitting in the corner with widened eyes. Scott was trying to scoot away. He was frightened at what he had just witnessed.

"Don't be afraid," Marcel told the boy, "I'm not here to hurt you. Let me untie you and get you out of here."

"My sister, she's in the office with Mr. Butler. He's going to hurt her."

"Let's get you out of here Scott, my brother Julian will get your sister out."

Arnaud and Andre were chasing Bill down while Jade and Rowena caught up with Charlie. Colin started running through the warehouse and began turning over barrels. He lit a match and threw it to the floor, then ran as flames started to spread throughout the rear of the warehouse. Giles jumped out of the office and started to run, but didn't get far, Nicky caught him, picked him up by the throat and threw him twenty feet away, causing him to hit his head on the concrete.

Julian yelled out for Trinity, but she didn't answer. The smoke and flames were filling the place and he had to get to her quick. Colin made his way to the office; he saw that Trinity was in there alone and untied her legs from the chair, but left her hands tied behind her.

"Well, darling, I'm not going to be able to get the revenge I wanted it seems, so I'll just have to settle for killing you." He didn't get to finish the rest of what he was about to say. Colin noticed that Julian had stepped into the office and quickly grabbed him before he had a chance to run and they began to fight. They were so fast she couldn't keep up with their movements. Colin broke free and ran from the office, leaving Trinity and Julian trapped. The fire was spreading rapidly throughout the warehouse and nearing the office.

Trinity remembered that this is what she saw in her dreams. She started to panic, the fire was coming so close to them, smoke had already flooded the office. Julian's voice was soft and soothing.

"Calm down Trinity, don't panic. We will get out of here, together." Julian untied her and stood her up, grabbing her arm to steady her and they rushed from the office toward the front of the building. They heard someone approaching and ducked behind a row of barrels.

"Stay here, I'll be right back," Julian told her. The back of the warehouse was fully engulfed in fire; barrels were shooting into the air; the entire place would be ashes soon. Trinity peeked out from behind the barrels and saw Colin looking around then dropping to the floor with his face in his hands. He must have found his father, she thought. She tried not to move, but slipped. Her hands flailed in the air to catch something to hold on to, anything and not be heard, but it was too late. He heard her and yelled out, "I'm coming for you Trinity!"

Marcel and the others were gathered out by their cars. Scott was sitting on the curb. They were waiting for some sign of Trinity and Julian; it had been thirty minutes since they regrouped. The entire warehouse was now engulfed in flames and they could hear sirens in the distance. They needed to get out of the area before those sirens got any closer.

"I'm going in, I've got to find my brother," Marcel told the group.

"No cousin, we are all going," Nicky said. They left Scott locked in Marcel's car, and headed back toward the warehouse.

Trinity saw Colin heading toward her with something in his hand. She couldn't make out what it was. Just then, Julian appeared and bent down to pick her up when Colin ran up on him. Trinity looked up just in time to see him coming toward Julian with what appeared to be a knife in his right hand. She screamed as he tried to plunge the knife into Julian's back. Trinity heard other footsteps descending upon them and yelled, as loud as she could. Rowena reached them first, her fangs were fully extended and her mouth was wide open, she grabbed Colin and spun him around. His eyes bucked wide. He couldn't believe what he was seeing. He tried with all his might to get away, to no avail. Rowena unarmed him so quickly and latched on to his neck before he could make a sound. Colin hit the floor and slumped into a heap.

Julian picked Trinity up off the floor and started running with her in his arms. They all rushed from the building just before it exploded. Everyone made it to their cars and sped away, just as the fire department and local authorities reached the scene.

Marcel and the rest of the group reached the mansion in record time, the sun was about to come up. Scott was reunited with his sister, who inspected him to make sure he was not hurt then she cried as they held on to each other. After things settled down, she turned to Julian and asked if there was something that he could do about Scott's memory being wiped. She didn't want her brother to remember any of this. She knew that she would have to explain some things to him, but not now, not today. Her brother knew what they were. He had seen their fangs; he saw Marcel drink blood. She didn't want him to tell anyone about that. Their secret needed to be kept safe and it wouldn't be if he told anyone.

"Whatever you do has to include Simon and Alex. I have to get the note so there is no trace of any of this," Trinity pleaded.

"We'll take care of it this evening," Nicky chimed in. "In the meantime, you and Scott can stay here. I'll order some nourishment for you and the boy."

Trinity needed time alone—to reflect on what had happened—she went up to Julian's bedroom, away from the others. She wondered about Colin and his father and how Mrs. Butler was going to deal with their disappearances. She also had to figure out how she was going to handle questions from her best friends. She had a lot to ponder and very little time to come up with answers.

"Sleep, I need to sleep, and then maybe things will become clearer to me", Trinity said out loud.

It was just after sundown when Trinity awoke from a deep sleep without screaming from the terrifying dreams she had been having. The house came alive. Everyone gathered in the study; Nicky passed the phone to Scott, at his request so he could call his brother and let him know that he and Trinity were fine and for Simon and Alex to come to where they were staying.

Trinity came downstairs just as Scott was finishing up his conversation with their brother. The time seemed to pass by slowly, while waiting for her brother Simon and his girlfriend Alex. A half hour passed and then doorbell rang, Rowena answered the door and ushered Alex and Simon into the study. The three siblings and Alex hugged. Once the reunion was over, they all took a seat as Marcel began to speak.

"There is much to be explained, and you are definitely owed an explanation, however, we will not be able to give you one at this time." As he was speaking, the lights in the house went dim and all seemed very quiet and still. The Simon, Scott and Alex were placed in a trance and when it was over, they awoke and was void of the knowledge of what had transpired within the last few hours. Scott seemed to think they had gathered to meet his sister's new beau and his family. After introductions were made again, Simon decided it was time to head back to the city. They kissed their sister again before leaving; then Simon and Alex left for home with Scott following slowly out the door behind them.

Trinity knew the minute her phone rang who it was. She didn't want to talk just then. She would wait until she was back in the apartment before she said anything. Julian walked up to her. They stared into each other's eyes for what seemed like an eternity.

"I'm crazy in love with you, my lady," Julian said.

"And I love you, big boy," Trinity answered.

"What are we to do then because I don't want to be without you Julian?"

"First, you can drop that pet name you gave me."

"Okay, but you are a big one," Trinity said with a smile.

"I'm not a boy," Trinity!

"Second, will you marry me the traditional way, and in vampire tradition?"

"If you're asking, Julian, ask me in the traditional way."

Everyone came into foyer just as Julian was getting down on one knee and taking Trinity's hand. He asked for her hand in marriage the traditional way, and as she said yes, he placed the most spectacular sapphire and diamond ring on her finger. Rising to a thunderous applause, he pulled Trinity into his arms and kissed her with all that he was and all that he had. "You're mine. You will always be mine. I'll always love you and I'll always be here to protect you and our young, should you choose to have them."

Trinity gasped. "You're going to let me remain a human?"

"Yes"! We will blood mate after the traditional ceremony. You will drink my blood and I will drink from you and only you. As long as I am around, you will never grow old. You won't be immortal, but you'll be pretty close to it. I want a family with you, my love."

"I want that too, Julian. I want to be with you always."

Julian came down hard on her lips again. He broke the kiss when he felt claps on the back from his brother and cousin, while the others shouted out their congratulations.

Julian stared back into Trinity's eyes and said, "Let's go back upstairs and practice making a baby." Trinity hit him on the shoulder as Nicky and the others laughed. Julian was in such a rush to get upstairs, he picked Trinity up and seemed to be flying, though she thought that was impossible. He went through the bedroom door as though the hounds of hell were on his heels. Ripping his shirt off, and pulling his pants down with lightening speed, he jumped on the bed took one look at his bride to be.

"Will you let me help you get undressed because you have too many clothes on right now?" Trinity chuckled and then nooded. "Please hurry; I want to be inside of you."

"Baby, your wish is my command," Trinity answered.

Julian could smell her arousal, the familiar soft aroma of lilacs. After the pants and thong and the top came off, he just ripped her bra off and palmed her breasts in his hands, playing with the soft buds until they pebbled from his touch. Her heart was kicking into overdrive. She wanted his bite, now.

"Take me Julian, please."

"I want to feel you inside me."

He took a hard pebble into his mouth and began to suck, laving all around the nipple then releasing it from his mouth only to replace it with the other one. Julian licked and sucked on the rosy pebble while Trinity moaned and pulled at the sheets. She twisted and wiggled her bottom while trying not to combust at the feel of his mouth on her nipples. He licked his way down her stomach to her slit. Once there, he used his tongue to open her slit and lick her clit. Julian gave her another sensation. He licked from her clit to the little pucker at the back of her. He latched onto her clit and sucked while he inserted a finger into her pussy. Trinity was so wet, she bucked as he sucked and finger fucked her. Julian inserted another finger and felt her G-Spot. He pumped his fingers and sucked harder, feeling her arch up off the bed she clamped her legs around his head and screamed his name with her release. He didn't let her rest, he withdrew his fingers and licked her juice off, then inserted one back into her getting it well lubricated, he began to suck her clit again as he eased his finger into her little puckered hole. Trinity's whole body lit up with the feel of what was happening to her.

"More, Julian. I want more."

He pushed in and out of her rectum with his finger while sucking on her clit. She moaned and reached down to pull on his hair. Julian groaned. He liked when she pulled his hair while his head was between her legs. He was fully aroused and wanted inside of her. He didn't care which hole she let him into as long as she let him in one of them. Another orgasm shot through her while she was getting plugged from behind with his thick finger.

He released her clit and withdrew his finger at the same time, leaving Trinity with an empty feeling. Julian turned her over and quickly positioned himself at her ass, ready to enter. "If this hurts, let me know and I will stop." Julian lubricated her behind with her juices while she held her cheeks open. His head of his cock pushed through the rim. She was so tight he thought he would have to stop.

"Go on, I can take it."

"I don't want to hurt you."

Just as he got the words out of his mouth, she held on to the bed and pushed back on him. The sound that came from him was inhuman. He had to sit still or else he would release before getting started. He gritted his teeth and began to slowly pump into her. Julian picked up the pace; he grabbed a hand full of hair and rode her like a champion. He reached around her and took a nipple in his hand just as Trinity reached down between her legs and started stimulating her clit. With her ass backed up on his dick, she could feel Julian pumping in and out, his balls slapping her ass; Trinity yelled out "Bite me, Julian." He stiffened, sweat beading on her back and his brow and upper lip. He lowered his head then licked her neck, his fangs extended and he bit down. The taste of her blood was intense, euphoric and wonderful as it went down his throat. He felt as though he was floating; he moaned as he drank. This was what he wanted. This was what he needed. He would never let her go. MINE, he thought. She screamed as she climaxed a third time, and took him over the cliff with her while his fangs were still in her neck. Julian released her neck and licked the puncture marks to seal them. They collapsed in a heap and lay there panting in each other's arms. They gently kissed each other, no words were necessary.

"It's time for me to go back to Lisa and Sara's apartment and get ready for my shift," Trinity said.

"Stay here with us, with me."

"I can't Julian, I have some explaining to do."

"Then I'll drive you and stay with you while you explain to your friends."

There was a strange smile on his face that she didn't understand. She wasn't sure she wanted to know the answer if she asked why he was smiling.

"I'll just shower and get dressed."

"I'll shower with you my lady."

When Julian and Trinity came downstairs, they found the house empty. Everyone else had already left for the Palace. They kissed once more then headed out the door.

Chapter 8

The drive back into the city was not long enough for Trinity. She didn't know how she was going to explain about her brother's kidnapping or the fact that Giles was Colin's father or anything else about the last 24-hours. She definitely couldn't let on about Julian and Marcel or the rest of the staff of the Palace being vampires. Her friends would think she was crazy.

Sara happened to be looking out her living room window when she spotted Julian's car. She ran for the front door and snatched it open before they had even gotten out of the car. Lisa was right behind her, yelling her name as they ran up to the car. Lisa in tears, they were glad to see her in one piece. They acknowledged Julian's presence while pulling Trinity in the house.

"How are you Sara asked with worry on her face?"

"When you didn't come home, we were worried until the two A's stopped by and filled us in on what happened with your brother being kidnapped," Lisa said.

"The two A's?" Julian said.

"Yes, Andre and Arnaud," Lisa answered.

"They told us everything, and when I say everything, I mean everything."

"Lisa, what are you talking about?" Trinity asked.

"We know about Colin and his father and that they wanted to kill you over your father's company. Andre went on to tell us about the unfortunate ending of everyone involved," Lisa added.

"It seems that my friends have told you ladies quite a bit," Julian remarked.

"Is that all they told you?" Trinity asked.

"No, not quite." We're waiting for you to tell us if you've set a date for the wedding," Sara said.

Trinity showed her friends her ring. They jumped and screamed hugging each other then they kissed Julian on the cheek. "I expect you to take good care of her and Lisa and I hope to be godmother to your children," Sara said.

"So, when is the wedding and are we planning it? Lisa asked.

"Both of you are going to be my maids of honor, and the wedding is in three weeks from Saturday," Trinity said.

The three of them cackled with glee as Julian just shook his head and laughed. "What's so funny Julian?" Trinity asked. "Oh, nothing, I was just wondering if I get to have a say in any of this." Julian said.

"Yeah, I Do," Sara said. They all laughed at Sara's comment. Let's go ladies. I'm taking you all to work tonight. We can have some champagne later.

Two days after the kidnapping, life went on as usual for the Parker family. There was nothing in the newspaper about Colin or his father Giles. There was a small article on the horrific fire in the warehouse district and that the bodies of two unidentified men were found not far from the burned warehouse. They had no identification on them. There was no mention of them being drained of blood.

That chapter of Trinity's life has closed and another is about to begin with Julian and hopefully a family of their own.

The Palace was closed to the public this night. The entire staff decorated the first floor for the festivities, which would be taking place in two hours. The tables were moved to the back out of the way and chairs were placed to the side. Everything was draped in black and white. Soft white lights twinkled from the ceiling and decorated the bar. Family, friends and invited guests arrived on time and were seated.

The groomsmen and bride's maids were in place followed by the maids-honor. Trinity wished her parents were alive so that they could be there and her father walk her down the aisle. She was wiping away her tears as her brother walked into the office. He knew the reason for her tears and kissed her on the cheek.

Trinity stepped into the room on the arm of her brother Simon. She was all smiles now as she walked toward the tall handsome figure dressed in a black tuxedo. Their eyes met and she started to well up again. She looked beautiful in her strapless black and white gown. She wore her hair up off her shoulders, which showed off her long neck and alabaster skin. The matching vale was adorned with diamonds and sapphires to match her ring and the teardrop necklace fell slightly in the crevasse of her breasts. Julian and Trinity faced each other and took their vows and after being pronounced married, they passionately kissed, only breaking because Marcel tapped Jules on the shoulder and said "save it for the bedroom brother." The room erupted into laughter after his comment.

The band played as people ate and drank; well all the humans ate anyway. Toasts were made to the happy couple. Trinity and Julian saw Tristan Winslow coming toward them smiling and reaching out to shake Jules' hand. "Thank you my friend, for all that you did for my wife." "Has there been any word from Andrea Campbell?"

"No, nothing, not even a trace that she ever existed," Tristan answered.

"I'll dig a little further to see if I can find out anything. In the meantime, Tristan watch your back."

"I will and you two as well, now, lets party."

The happy couple walked out on the dance floor for their first dance as the band played a slow song, requests were taken from the guests after their dance. The band played an upbeat song that Trinity loved; Two to Tango by Vanessa Daou. Trinity had a surprised look on her face when she saw Julian take to the stage with the band. He sang a loving ballad to her. Sara and Lisa turned and smiled at their friend who was tearing up at the song being sung. When he stepped down from the stage and took Trinity in his arms, she couldn't help herself, she was so happy; she started to cry. His eyebrows creased together as he stared down at her. I hope my singing wasn't that bad. She burst into a full blown fit of crying by then. Julian held her tight as he walked her back to the office to comfort his bride.

"Trinity, tell me why you cry."

"Oh, Julian, I'm just so happy and I love you so much that I can't help but think that something is going to come along and, and spoil it."

"I never want to be without you."

Julian's eyes crinkled and his lips turned up into a wide smile. "I love you too baby and you will always have me. Lets go home baby so I can make you mine forever."

"Yes Julian, my love, yours forever."

The story continues

ABOUT THE AUTHOR:

A. R. Flowers, better known to her friends as Allie loves spending time with family and friends and her cat Scruffie; taking walks, playing acoustic guitar, riding her Harley and is a football fanatic.

Allie has been writing since 1987, starting with children's books and then romance although her first love has been paranormal.

BOOKS:

FORBIDDEN KISS (Julian's Mate)

A GIFT OF LOVE My Vampire's Valentine (Novella)

HERS TO PROTECT-- Rowena's Story coming soon

THE VAMPIRE'S OBSESSION coming soon